SECRET AGENT OF GOD

Eileen Slovak

All Biblical quotes noted in this work of fiction came from the King James Version of The Holy Bible.

Copyright © 2013 Eileen Slovak
All rights reserved.

ISBN: 1492868191
ISBN 13: 9781492868194
Library of Congress Control Number: 2013922438
CreateSpace Independent Publishing Platform
North Charleston, South Carolina

I dedicate this novel to Nick, Nicholas and Katherine for their infinite patience with my obsessive drive to write.

With many thanks to: Writers by the Bay, the crew of MustGetBeers, Kerry Caparco, Kristin Corcoran, Lisa Deiranieh, Maureen Goodwin, Dodi Heywood, Harriet McGuire, Kristina Slovak, Renee Stone and Catherine Walton. With sincere gratitude to all who were Twitter, Wordpress and Facebook fans prior to this publication and to Createspace.com, the Fox News Channel, and the Catholic Church.

CHAPTER ONE
Genesis

And the Angel of God spake unto me in a dream…
And I said, Here am I. —Genesis 31:11, KJV

So, I'm stuck in this vehicle trying to get my hands loose, but I'm not having any luck. Whoever grabbed me taped my mouth shut, slapped a blindfold on me, and tied my hands to my feet. I'm more or less hog-tied, and I can hardly budge. Some foreigner asked me for directions. Someone else grabbed me from behind. The rest is fuzzy. Apologies in advance; I ramble when I'm nervous.

Shit! Why in the hell did I give up swearing? I might need to take it up again. The mother-effers must have used something on me. My head feels like it might split wide open. I don't remember anything hitting me.

With the tires thumping, it sounds like my face is right up on the road and it's making me sick to my stomach. If I throw up with duct tape on my mouth, I'll surely choke to death, so I'm fighting it down. I'm trying to stay calm and figure out what happened. Breathing through your nose is harder than you'd think.

Breathe, damn it.

I heard about a woman stuffed in a trunk who kicked out the taillight and stuck her hand out the hole so other drivers could see her. At least I'm not in a trunk. If I wiggle around, I don't bump into anything. There are no insides to this thing. When I move, the rope gets tighter and cuts into my skin.

I hear two voices, but I can't make out what they're saying. They aren't speaking English or anything like it.

I wish they'd taped my nose instead of my mouth. It stinks in here like nasty sweaty socks, and there's something hard, wet, and sticky under my butt. My skin's as icy as the metal floor. I must be in a van of some sort.

I know what you're thinking, but it's not fear making me shiver. I guess I might be scared when my anger settles down. It helps I sense they're not planning to kill me, whoever *they* are. I'm thinking I did something I shouldn't have, and now I'm going to pay for it. I'm assuming its karma. You see, I *know* things before they happen, and that's likely how I ended up here. I'm still trying to get a handle on it all.

You're probably thinking then I should've seen this coming, but my second sight didn't bother to mention I was about to be effing abducted. The voices only tell me what they want me to know. It would feel good to cuss right now, but I gave it up for my daughter, Jessie.

Thankfully, Jessie wasn't with me when this happened. I can't stop fretting about her. After my shift ended at Safe Harbor, where I'm a certified nursing assistant, I went to pick Jessie up from The Sisters of Mercy—my holy day care. Sister Bridget takes great care of Jessie.

Bridget or like I call her, Bridge, is the youngest of the sisters. She's only twenty-four, three years older than I am. Maybe Jessie feels safe with Bridge because she's young like I am, only so much wiser. For too many reasons, I'd never make it as a nun. One time, I asked Bridge why she became one.

She said, "Quite simply, I heard the call and I answered it."

"What do you mean?" I asked. "Did God *call* you? 'Hey, Bridge. It's me, God. Pick up.'"

She laughed. "Yes. In a way, that's what happened."

"How does heaven make a call to earth?" I asked.

Bridge smiled with such brightness it was like looking at the sun. I swore I could see my own reflection in her icy blue eyes. Her skin was milky-white and she wore her long, brown hair in a braid down her back. I'd seen her in street clothes. She looked just like you and me—well, except that she was holier.

She said, "It's something you know right down to your toes. Truthfully, Janice, this is everything I've ever wanted. I'm secure in the knowledge that I'm on the right and true path."

Can you imagine being so certain your life is on track? I sure can't. Maybe that's always been my problem.

I do know that my arms miss holding Jessie, and it hurts just to think about her tiny face. I'm supposed to take care of her and keep her safe, but now look at the fix I'm in here. What if these goons get Jessie too?

If Bridge sees my car out in front of the rectory and there's no sign of me, I hope she'll call the cops. She has to know I'd never just leave Jessie, doesn't she? I expect she'll pray for me anyhow.

Where are these clowns taking me? I have to focus. *Calm down, Janice Morrison. Pray and think. Pray and think. What did you do?*

Prayer is the only thing that calms my nerves anymore, but it wasn't always that way. For most of my life, I've been a sinner. It was bound to catch up with me.

Even though I fight it, I must take after my mom, Dee. She named me after Janice Joplin, the singer. All I know is that Dee was disappointed when I wasn't a boy because she wanted to name me James or Jim, after a different singer, Jim Morrison. My friends don't even know who either of those singers is so I've stopped telling most people that story. Both of them died young from drugs or alcohol.

I don't drink much. Pot puts me to sleep, so what's the draw there? I tried hallucinogenic mushrooms once, but didn't take to them. That was enough for me. I like being in control. That's how I'm different from Dee.

Focus on breathing, Janice. Breathe in. Breathe out.

I can't wait for karma to kick some kidnapper butt. Where was I? Oh, yeah, if only I could forget. *Dee* is short for *Deirdre*. She's a thirty-eight-year-old singer and a drunken slut. It's a sin to speak ill of your parents, so I rarely talk about her at all. My grandmother raised me after Dee ran off with some guitarist. From what I've heard, she's been through a string of them since then.

After my fifth birthday, Gram wouldn't let Dee see me anymore. I found a picture of my five-year-old self wearing a frilly little dress, sitting with a half eaten birthday cake with tears running down my face. Dee was in the background with some guy. They were both probably high. Gram said Dee and her friend ate the cake before I'd even blown out the candles. Then Dee and Gram got in a wicked fight. I don't remember any of it, but Gram told me, "There were things said that can never be unsaid."

I always expected Dee would come back for me. I've learned most of what I know about her from Gram and from rumors around town. I imagined the rest from growing up in Dee's room at Gram's house. Under the bed, I found a box of Dee's things. There was a mood ring, a pet rock, and a few pictures of her with boyfriends. There was nothing racy. Really, she might have been a normal teenager before she had me.

I have Dee's thick, blond, wavy hair. She styled hers to look like the poster of Farah Fawcett-Majors that I found in the bedroom closet. I kept it. It sounds weird, but when I was young, it was like having a small piece of my mom.

Wait a minute. We're slowing down and stopping. Nope. Maybe we're at a red light. I can still hear them chattering like a couple of squirrels. What is this language? It's not Spanish. Maybe it's Greek.

I've read—I read constantly—that your mind forgets on purpose to protect itself from harmful memories. I believe this is true.

Of course, I believe in a lot of weird stuff now. Life has a funny way of working out. According to Gram, I was God's way of giving her a second chance to raise a child properly. I only hope I didn't let her down after everything that happened.

I lived with Gram up until I graduated from high school and couldn't take it anymore. I was too old to be living with my grandma and got tired of sneaking out whenever I wanted to see a guy. That and she was always criticizing my clothes.

"Janice, how can you breathe in those dungarees? They look too tight. It must be painful to wear them. And what's that on your face? Is that rouge?"

They're called jeans, Gram. And no one calls it rouge anymore.

"It's all right, Gram. I'll take care of myself. Don't I always?"

❖

The trouble began with the second sight, which is usually sort of a puzzle. About a year ago, I started waking up at 3:00 a.m. every night. My body's internal alarm clock was just ringing away. I was having strange thoughts and seeing pictures in my head—pictures of people I didn't know. I thought I was hallucinating, and wondered if the drugs my mother had taken were still swimming through my veins.

Anyway, it's amazing how far I've come since I had my first visions, before the messages became crystal clear and before Jessie was born. Sometimes, I feel like going back in time.

The van is slowing down. I hear gravel crunching under the tires. We've stopped. *Erk. Week. Wump.* They get out and slam the doors. I hear their muffled voices outside, and another voice joins in. They're talking faster and in short bursts, like fighting. It sounds almost sounds tribal. Keys are dangling outside the van.

Shit! Sorry. I have to cuss.

Weeerp. Another door opens. Whoa! A blast of cold air hits me like a slap in the face. I'm shivering harder now. A bright light slips through the blindfold, but I can't make anything out. I'm pretending to be asleep while the three voices keep jabbering.

The floor bounces. I hear boots on metal coming toward me. Someone with rough hands grabs my feet and drags me into the light. He scoops me up like a bride and then tosses me around like a ragdoll. He smells like cigarettes, onions, and sweat. His body's soft, but his grip is strong like an ape.

Now they've all gone quiet. I can't hear any street noises either, only crickets and shoes scratching on the gravel. Where in the hell are we?

He jostles me around. *Bump. Bump.* It feels like we're going up stairs. *Erk. Keek. Wump.* A door opens and closes again. The light vanishes. It's warm now, but I'm still shaking. The ape carries me a few more steps and then stops. Light slips through the blindfold again, but not enough to see.

A new voice argues with the ape. Ape's voice is louder. While they go at it, he's standing still and holding me. Then he moves again. There's a hollow *pop* and a *wump*. Another door opens. He takes a few steps and then lowers me onto something soft—a bed.

I hear footsteps moving away. *Slam. Click. Click.* A key locks the door from the outside. It's dark and too warm in here. My stomach wants to wretch. My heart beats so hard I feel it pulsing in my ears. Outside the door, they start babbling again.

Who are these bastards, anyway? What do they want? Are they going to rape me? Please, voices from above, give me something, some kind of sign. God, please give me the strength to handle whatever's coming next.

CHAPTER TWO
Inclement

I must have passed out. Finally, one of the em-effers is back to untie me. It's about damn time. I nearly peed myself. He doesn't say a word. He smells like soap and spices, a different scent than Ape unless Ape showered. No. This one has softer hands, not sandpapery mitts like Apes. I'm stiff from lying in one position for so long. All I want to do is stretch and get some feeling back into my legs. Then he goes and reties my wrists in the front. Genius! I might have to call him that.

He pushes me forward and grabs my arm, leading me somewhere. Maybe he's taking me to my execution. I hope he's taking me to the bathroom. I hear faint music coming from another part of the building, no lyrics, just instruments. *Creak*. A door opens. He shoves me, flicks on a light, and shuts the door. Still blindfolded, I stagger forward and nearly trip over a toilet. I don't know about you, but I like to see when I'm peeing.

It's a challenge going to the bathroom with your hands tied together especially when you're wearing a flipping blindfold. I have new respect for the blind. With my fingertips, I push the blindfold up a tiny bit. That's better.

I don't know how long I've got so I focus on peeing. My darn scrubs are hard to pull down with these wrist ties. When I plunk down on the toilet, I see that my undies are damp. Damn.

It isn't the worst bathroom I've ever seen a bunch of guys share. I mean, I didn't hear any female voices. The bathroom looks clean but it's nothing fancy with puke-pink tile from the 1980's and a plain white toilet, sink, and a shower. There's a window but they covered it up in black paper.

I guess he thinks I'm taking too long. He starts pounding on the door. I try to shout, "Hold your damn horses! You try peeing without hands!"

With the tape on my mouth, all I can do is mumble. I flush, pull myself together, attempt to wash my hands, and fumble with the doorknob. He knocks. I knock back to show him that I'm done. The door opens a crack, and I hear music, louder now. It's rock music. Led Zeppelin.

"Keep the blindfold on," he says through the gap.

I fix the blindfold and tap on the door again.

When I step out he touches my face and I jump on instinct. In one quick movement, he rips the tape off my face. Son of a...I'm glad I didn't see that coming.

"No screaming or it goes back on. Understand?"

I nod. He grabs my arm again, drags me back to the room I came from, shoves me in, and locks the door again. I push up the blindfold, but everything is still pitch black. A crack of light comes in from under the door and it takes my eyes a minute to adjust. The walls are close. It's some sort of closet. There are no windows. I can make out the shadowy shapes of the bed, a chair, and some cardboard boxes stacked in the corner. I can't see anything else. I wonder if there are any spiders in here.

I move around slowly in the dark and sit on the edge of the bed. I'm steamed now. The jerk who took me to the bathroom spoke fancy English—the kind they use in England. Still I know it wasn't my imagination before, they were definitely speaking a foreign language. I'll call him English. His voice this way is familiar. He was the one who asked me for directions right before I parked behind that white van—some sort of utility truck. I don't remember what state was on the license plate or if it was local from Maryland or not.

I'm trying to remember his face. It'll come to me. What exactly did he say? It was something like, "Miss, I wonder if you can help me."

This is what I get for being a Good Samaritan. Why take me? Was it something I saw? I'm missing a connection here. They surely don't plan to use me for ransom since Jessie's all I have of value, and they didn't take her, yet.

Jessie.

Having a baby wasn't exactly in my plans. I know I sound ungrateful. I remember the day I had to tell Gram I was pregnant. I dreaded what she'd say. Especially since, up until that point she'd kept me from following in Dees' footsteps. I imagine Gram thought we were in the clear.

I know Gram spent more time in her chapel room praying for me than for anything else. The chapel was what we called the TV room. Gram needed the space for all of her statues, her pictures of the holy family, and her bibles. Yes, she had a collection of bibles. It was a better use of the room since we only owned one small thirteen-inch TV, and we watched it in the kitchen. Gram didn't let me watch much though, since there was nothing on but 'filth and trash'. On Sunday afternoons, when the weather was inclement, she let me watch old movies, and religious programs.

I like the word *inclement*. Every day, I work on my vocabulary by learning the meaning of at least one new word. Most people don't know you can build a stellar vocabulary that way. *Conception*, *expecting*, *responsibility*—right now these are the words swirling around in my brain.

After the fateful night I got pregnant, I rarely saw Jessie's father. It was odd, considering how intimate we'd been to conceive Jessie in the first place. Of course, given the chance he'd still be taking advantage of me. Later, when I was six months pregnant, I saw him at a funeral. He wanted to get together again, and it wasn't as though I could get any more pregnant. In the past, I've made the same stupid mistakes over again, but that time, I declined. He was a pig. I'll never know how I let my guard down with that creep in the first place. That's me, always turning a blind eye onto other people's faults. Even though I know it's wrong, I confess I wished Jason dead that day.

Bridge always says, "Be careful, because the things you think about sometimes come true."

Who needs such a heavy weight on their soul? Bridge is like my spiritual guide. Based on our discussions, I have plenty of soul cleansing to do. I may eventually get around to forgiveness or not. I'm in no particular hurry to decide. Jason is a selfish, spoiled, and conceited rich kid. Why should I forgive him anyway?

When we met, I was working for Dick and Claire O'Neil at their mansion in Annapolis and taking care of Claire's mother-in-law, Nanny. It was a whole lot easier than my regular CNA gig at Safe Harbor in Churchton, Maryland. Safe Harbor is an assisted living facility—I mean residence. They don't like when you refer to it as a facility. It sounds too institutionalized. I still work there in the afternoons. Well, at least I did, before this happened.

What can I say? It's not glamorous but it pays the bills. I spend my days emptying bedpans, taking vitals, and carting around trays of unappetizing food. It's thrilling, all right.

At the time, I'd been working my tail off for two years. My supervisor, Melanie Golden, liked me. So when the O'Neil job came up, she recommended me and reworked the schedule so I could do both jobs. Each morning, from eight until noon, I worked at the O'Neil house. Then I ate my sack lunch on the twenty-minute ride back to Safe Harbor and worked my shift there until 8:30 p.m. The days were long, but I was making twice my usual pay.

I haven't quite figured Ms. Golden out yet. She's a fiercely private person. Everyone calls her Mel because she's somewhat masculine in her features, even though she has a rocking body. I wish I had her curves. I'm built more like a teenage boy. Finally, after I had Jessie, though, I got a little something more up top.

It's funny. Mel gave me the hardest time about being pregnant. When I told Mel about the baby, she was furious. She said, "I thought you were smart, Janice."

Me too, but apparently I'm not. If only I knew then, what I know now. Do you see what I mean about the *premonitions*? It's selective knowledge. I'm sure there's a reason. Like, if I knew what was coming, I might never have worked for the O'Neil family and then I wouldn't have had Jessie. Technically, the Sisters of Mercy have her right now, but I'll get back to her. I don't know how I'll do it, but I will.

Around when the *fit hit the shan*, Jason O'Neil was home on Christmas break from Georgetown. It might have been the beautiful, festive decorations in their gorgeous home. I don't know what it was. I only know I let myself falter.

The kitchen of the O'Neil home cost more than Gram's cottage in North Beach where I grew up. I know because I heard Claire O'Neil complaining about the renovations. She was unsatisfied with the custom cherry cabinets and the imported teak floor. As it turned out, the granite countertops, specially made and imported from Italy, were the exact same one's Claire's neighbor had. That ticked Claire off and she gave the contractor a reaming over the phone.

A person could get lost in the O'Neil's doublewide refrigerator. To store extra food for all of the parties they threw, they had a second refrigerator in the mudroom. I'm certain the kitchen alone was bigger than my whole apartment.

Nancy O'Neil or Nanny had a stroke that had paralyzed the left side of her body. She needed help with feeding, changing, and companionship. Those were my main duties. Nanny was supposed to exercise her nonfunctioning side. This was just a cruel thing to do. Whenever the physical therapist came, Nanny would get this panicked look on the functioning side of her face. Her progress was pathetic; it was enough to break your heart.

What amazed me the most was how determined she was to look neat and tidy. I'd brush her hair and put her makeup on for her. The eyeliner was a challenge. The wrinkled skin around her eyes moved too much, making the liner smudge. She was the picture of patience through it all. I could see that fire lived on in those green eyes of hers.

I did my job and apologized whenever I changed the sheets or bathed Nanny. She was a bony little thing and no more than seventy pounds. You'd be surprised how hard it is to shift that much weight on your own. There's a technique to it. First, you prop the patient up onto pillows. Then, you tuck the sheets under, and repeat the same process on the other side. Believe me you build up some muscles that way. I can honestly say I've never dropped anyone, and I've had experience with all kinds of people. I'd have taken a dozen patients like Nanny.

One day she had all the photos albums out. Dick O'Neil, her son, must have done it. He was good that way. Nanny pointed to people in the photographs and told me about them.

"Thers Dicky and thas Jazon. Tho prezious." The stroke made her sound like Sylvester from the Tweety-Bird cartoon, but I could understand her.

"That's Jason? Well, he sure was a cute little baby." *Darn pity he hadn't stayed that way.*

"And Rishard," she pointed at a man who looked like her son Dick, Claire's husband, but the photo was in black and white. It must have been Nanny's husband Dick Sr. She touched the picture, as if she could still feel him. Even her good hand was so shaky and transparent that all of the veins were on display like the map of an ancient city. Dick Jr. and Dick Sr. were both surgeons, but Dick Sr. had died of a heart attack four years prior. God bless him.

Hold on. I have to bless myself. Damn wrist ties and would it kill them to bring me some water? I'm almost out of spit here! I can't hear anything out there. I wonder if they left. I try the door, but they locked it. With my ear pressed to it, I can hear voices. They're English voices. It sounds like television. Man, I'm starving. I wish they'd get on with it. The worst part is the waiting and the wondering.

Where was I? Oh, I never did see much of Dick. He worked insane hours at the hospital. Claire was the one I worked for and she was wicked, to put it plainly. She acted sweet on the rare occasions when Dick was around. When he wasn't there, that's when I had to look out. If you ask me, Claire was the real dick. That's probably where Jason got his attitude.

Claire was even mean to Nanny's dog, Francis. I'd catch her yelling at him and pushing him outside with her high-heel. He was a Schnauzer named after St. Francis of Assisi, the patron saint of animals. Claire had no right to mistreat him. I could tell Nanny had no love for Claire either. She made faces whenever Claire was hovering around and pretending to care.

"Nanny, let's get you some fresh pillows. Won't that be nice?" Claire said.

Somehow, all of her supposedly nice ideas meant more work for me.

"Janice, be a dear and go fetch some pillows from the linen closet."

She said *fetch* as if I was Francis or something.

Whenever Claire left to go shopping, get her hair done, or do whatever she did all day, I'd sneak down and let Francis in. First, I'd set a bone down on the Oriental rug for him to munch on. Then I'd bring him up to see Nanny. I tried not to think about what would happen to poor old Francis when Nanny passed away.

If humans were dogs, Claire would be a bloodhound. Whenever I went to the bathroom or took a short break with Stefania Fortini, the cook and housekeeper, Claire would always hunt me down.

"Oh, there you are," she'd say, flashing her big phony smile and showing off her fangs. She'd act as if I'd been gone for hours instead of a few seconds.

Claire knew how to push Stefania's buttons too.

"Stefania, this sauce tastes very salty. You know salt isn't good for Richard's blood pressure."

"Si, Signora O'Neil. E il prosciutto, non sale."

"Well, it tastes like salt to me. I'm afraid you'll need to fix something else."

"Strega, uscire dalla mia cucina," Stefania said, meaning 'witch, get out of my kitchen.'"

"Pardon me?" Claire asked.

"Si, Signora O'Neil."

The greatest contributing factor to Stefania's ongoing employment was Claire's woeful understanding of the Italian language. Whenever Claire tried to speak Italian, she butchered it. I knew better. Stefania was prideful about two things: her language and her cooking. Anyone with any sense would know not to mess with either.

From working with Stefania, I learned I had a knack for languages. I added some Italian words to my routine of learning a new word every day. It took no time at all to learn some Italian cuss words and interesting phrases. It helped me curb my swearing habit too. Whenever I cussed in Italian, no one would know what it meant besides Stefania and me. Of course, my baby still might end up with a foreign potty mouth. I never claimed to be the perfect mom.

"You come with me to Italy next time, and you learn Italian like this." Stefania said snapping her fingers. "Look at me. I live here only a few years and my English is *perfetto*." Whenever she forgot the English word, she'd just throw in the Italian substitute instead. It worked.

Thinking about Stefania's cooking; my stomach makes noises I've never heard before. I was in such a hurry to pick Jessie up from daycare I skipped dinner. I wonder if they plan to starve me to death. Starvation must be a terrible way to die. I'm imagining the smells wafting up from the O'Neil's kitchen: garlic, sauces, and simmering stews. Mama Mia my belly aches.

When Claire was gone, I had the best times with Stefania. During our coffee and cigarette breaks, Stefania made espresso. Since it was stronger than American coffee, it helped me keep up with my work schedule. Claire had a restaurant-quality coffee machine, but Stefania used her own little metal pot she had brought from Naples, called a *Bialetti-Moka*. It looked old-fashioned but she said it was the best.

"Janeeze, you don't sip the espresso. You do like this," she said, tossing back her head and downing the whole thing in one shot. I envied her long, thick black hair and her confidence. She carried herself like a movie star.

While I filled a water glass, Stefania set up Nanny's lunch tray. She prepared a saucer of warm, homemade tomato soup. It was her family's recipe for pasta fagioli, with soft white beans, pasta, and something green floating around in it.

Some of Stefania's relatives still live in Naples where she said they made the best food in the world. Her parents, Maria and Vincenzo Fortini, owned a restaurant in Annapolis, Maryland called *Basilico* and several of her relatives worked there. She described them all so colorfully. Mostly, we talked about the big *festa* they had every year for the family on Christmas Eve.

"Your family must fill up the whole restaurant," I said.

"Yes, so now we have the *festa* at my parent's house and close *Basilico* for Christmas. Other years, customers kept coming and mamma didn't have the heart to send them away. It got too crazy."

"Isn't it a busy time to be closed?" I asked.

"Yes, but family comes first, before everything else. Besides, most of the family works at *Basilico*. My brother, Francesco, and my cousins, Maximus, Ciro and Enzo are the waiters. Everyone is at the *festa*, so we would have no one left to work."

The *festa* sounded so much more wonderful than my usual holiday plans. Gram and I always spent Christmas Day together. After Mass, we'd go back to her little house, exchange our gifts, and hang out.

Ever since I was little, Gram worked in the rectory on Christmas Eve. It was her job to take care of the bookkeeping for Saint Mary's church in North Beach, Maryland. She managed the finances, and helped with the preparations for all of the holy days. Every year, I went with her to decorate the church for Christmas, until I was old enough to stay home. Somehow, it was more magical to see it transformed on Christmas Day than it was to be part of the transformation crew.

Other than staying home alone with my miniature Christmas tree, I had no elaborate plans for Christmas Eve. My tree was no bigger than a branch on the O'Neil family's twelve-foot evergreen mountain in the middle of their elegant living room. The lights on their spruce shined like diamonds, and the most serene angel sat on top. Whenever I passed by it, I stared up at the angel's porcelain face. It might sound crazy, but I always thought she was watching over me.

CHAPTER THREE
Impetuous

Blessed are they which do hunger and thirst after righteousness: for they shall be filled. —Matthew 5:6, KJV

I've no idea how long I've been in this room. It does weird things to your mind spending too much time alone and my mind is already strange enough. I'm groggy like I've been up for hours. Even before this, I didn't sleep well.

Since my visions come just before I doze off, falling asleep is a cause for anxiety. I get these pictures of people in my head, random faces coming at me at an alarming rate. Like when Nanny was showing me her photographs. The only difference is that it's ten times faster and I can't focus on the images quite right. In the beginning, I just ignored them. I tried different sleep aids. Then the faces took on meaning in my everyday life.

I was unconscious for part of the drive, so I can't gauge how far away from home I am. Does it matter? I may as well be a million miles away. How will anyone ever find me? Did my captors leave any clues behind?

I'm trying to figure out if the drive was minutes or hours like that day I was with Stefania and we wound up lost and drove through the Harbor Tunnel in Baltimore. That day I had the worst premonition of them all.

There's no use; I can't gage the distance or the direction. In many ways, being in the dark is nerve-racking. We could be in Virginia, Northern Maryland, or anywhere. If English comes back, I'll just come right out and ask him where we are. I can be impetuous.

The music is playing again like an orchestra. It's so loud I hear it clear through the wall and I don't hear him coming. When he throws the door open, I startle. His voice is frosting smooth and sweet.

"I'm glad you're awake," English says.

"So, where are we? Why did you bring me here? What do you and your fellow thugs want with me?" I ask.

"Now you want to pretend to be ignorant? That's amusing to me, Janice. Think hard."

Really, I haven't a clue why I'm here. When he talks, his voice moves around. He's pacing back and forth in front of me.

"We both know you are not as innocent as you appear. I feel like we are alike in some ways. Although, I admit, what perplexed me was why you would make the mistake of becoming involved in things that are clearly none of your business. Do you want to know what I think? I think you cannot help yourself. We've been watching you for some time. Surprised? Such a creature of habit. Speaking of habits, I hope your friends, the nuns, aren't too surprised when we…"

I leap off the bed and lunge at him. With my hands tied, I'm pathetic. He just laughs and pushes me backward with one hand. I fall hard against the bed.

"Thank you, Janice. I needed a laugh this morning. There's no sense in getting ahead of ourselves. The future is uncertain, isn't it? If only I had a crystal ball to figure out what comes next. You put yourself in the middle of this, little American girl, so you are the only one to blame if it turns out poorly. I expect complete cooperation. Anything less will lead to…consequences. Understood?"

I nod.

"Good. Then you may stay alive for now. Please quit the act. The others don't have my level of patience."

The arrogant jerk slams the door behind him and leaves me with that. My impetuousness has gotten me nowhere in a hurry. I want to scream but it's against the rules. I don't like the way he says *American* like it's a bad word. I resent his whole stupid speech. Who does this idiot think he is? I'm not a girl. I have a child. My child is out there, while I'm in here—wherever the hell this is.

Come on, voices, tell me what they want? How many of them are there? How do I get out of this?

Still, he brings no water or food. I'd give anything for something to eat. I'd even take the bad hospital food we served at Safe Harbor.

Safe. I thought I was so safe in my little town. Nothing ever happens in North Beach, Maryland. My life was so boring before all of this, before the premonitions, before I got pregnant. I was saving for college. Education went the way of most of my plans. Money was tight after Rachel, my roommate, moved out and I was stuck paying all the rent.

Rachel was a junkie and ended up in rehab in Pennsylvania. We worked together before Mel fired Rachel for stealing drugs from the patients. Technically, assistants couldn't give meds, so I'm sure Rachel had help. Nurse Miller was supposed to keep track of all medications and lock the cage, but lazy as the day is long she was always giving her work away. Anyway, with Rachel gone, I had to move on. I had bills to pay.

Even worse, Rachel left me a cat named Rags. When you pick up Rags, he just hangs there boneless and soft like a fur pillow. He couldn't catch a mouse if you dragged it straight across his nose. Rachel declawed him, so he didn't go outside, which was a bummer for my work schedule. When Rags got lonesome, he liked to pee on my things. I eventually started letting him roam around the hall for exercise.

That's how he met and smoothed things over with Mrs. Sivkulanitz, my neighbor who lives in apartment fifteen across the hall. During one of Rachel's drunken stumbling incidents in the wee hours of the morning, she called Mrs. Sivkulanitz *old lady syphilis*.

After Rachel left, I started talking more to Mrs. Sivkulanitz or Mrs. S. for short and making small talk. Then, I noticed Rags would disappear into apartment fifteen. Sometimes he'd be gone for hours. Once I started working for the O'Neil's, I'd leave Rags with Mrs. S. all day. I think he liked her place better than mine because he got more attention and there were better places to hide. Our apartments are the same size, but hers seemed tiny crammed full of a lifetime of possessions. Once Rachel's things were gone, my apartment sort of echoed.

I offered to give Rags to Mrs. S. but she preferred our kitty daycare arrangement. It's weird how she's kinder than I thought. She's like having another grandmother and says things like, "Bless your heart, dear. You're an angel on earth."

Like Gram, when Mrs. S. gets hold of my ear she bends it.

"Janice," she said to me one day. "Why are you so skinny? Look at your clothes hanging off you. You don't eat the food I make for you?"

"I sure do. I just can't put on weight. That's the way it's always been."

She likes to poke my side with her bony finger.

"Meat," she said. "That's what you need to stick to those ribs."

"Maybe," I said. "But meat's pretty expensive these days."

Lying here, I'm wondering what it's like not to have to worry about how much everything costs all the time. If I had money like the O'Neil's, I'd go to the supermarket and fill my cart with steak, chicken, and ice cream—anything I wanted. I wouldn't even look at the prices. I'm not saying I've ever really starved. Gram made sure I ate. But living on my own, I struggled to pay the bills.

Right now, I'd settle for a piece of bread and some water. What kind of prison is this? I'm no criminal. I don't deserve this. There are criminals right now who are walking around as free as can be and living the good life like Jason O'Neil.

CHAPTER FOUR
Karma

For the month of December, Jason was home from college on Christmas break. I won't lie. He looked good. Even though I have to say, I couldn't see any of Dick or Claire in his sandy hair and hazel eyes. There was something not quite right about Jason. Whenever he wasn't out getting into trouble with his friends, he was hanging around the house and being a big pain in my butt.

"Hey, Janice, you're looking fine today. Here, let me help you with that."

"No thank you, Jason. I'm good."

"Come on. You work too hard. You can take a little break and talk to me for a minute."

"You know that I can't, Jason. Shouldn't you be out having fun with your friends?"

"I'd rather be with you."

"Well, I'm sorry. I have work to do," I said and then off I went.

Stefania told me he'd come on to her once. She let him have it right in the *pene*. That's her slang word for a man's privates. It seemed fitting, named after pasta.

The job at the O'Neil home paid pretty well and I needed the money, so I figured ignoring Jason was my best option. As it happened, he was more persistent than I'd thought he'd be. One day, he cornered me in the pantry and shoved his tongue down my throat.

Jason was good-looking, but Francis gave better kisses. I shoved him off me and told him so.

"I could have you fired," he said.

He was right, so I tried to be nice to him again.

"It's nothing personal, Jason. It's just that I'm a virgin and I'm saving myself."

Of course, this was a flat-out lie and my first mistake. How was I supposed to know he was a virgin slayer and by saying that I'd only egg him on more?

Stefania went off on me in Neapolitan for a good fifteen minutes when she found out I'd kissed him. She got over it but she warned me to watch out.

"He's a snake, Janeeze, and a snake doesn't change his spots. *Capito*?"

In truth, I was just a little bit lonely. The holidays always brought me down, and Jason was so darn persistent. I do believe in karma—you know what comes around goes around. All of my sins surely come back to bite me, and I can't be the only one. Here's hoping Jason gets his comeuppance someday.

Things were going along as normal as can be. I was managing to pay my bills and save some money with the extra I earned from working two jobs. For a spell, life was good. Then I let my guard down. I know, stupid me.

Dick and Claire planned to spend a long weekend in New York. To give them some privacy, Stefania always went home on weekends and helped in the restaurant. Dick and Claire couldn't leave Nanny alone with Jason because he was too irresponsible. OK, so this should have been a big clue. But they offered to pay me enough to cover a month's rent, so I said yes. Mel let me leave Safe Harbor early on Friday. When I got to the house, Jason was out with his pals.

After Dick and Claire left, I got Nanny settled and then set myself up in the guest room that was down the hall from her room. I felt like a princess surrounded by antiques and fine things. I might have enjoyed being a permanent guest at the O'Neil house. I could see why Stefania liked it.

I don't know why, but I locked the door. Something just told me to do it. I was so comfortable sleeping in the big queen-size bed. Rich people even have better sheets. I felt like I was like sleeping on a cloud. Snuggled down under the cozy down comforter, I floated off to sleep. I only woke up once at 2:00 a.m. when I pretended to not hear Jason clawing at my door.

On Saturday, I gave Nanny her sponge bath and checked her thoroughly for bedsores. Nanny was one of the lucky ones. She had a slew of doctors and a physical therapist. They made sure she moved around.

I held up the diaper and waggled it.

"I have to move you and do a change, Nanny."

"Awight, Dear."

When I rolled her over, I tried not to think about how much lighter she'd been getting. Old age was stealing the weight in her bones, along with her strength. As respectfully as possible, I changed her. Her hipbones poked unnaturally out of her pasty white skin. Afterward, I lifted her arms and legs, and moved them around slowly.

Then I noticed her wedding picture sitting on top of a box of her things next to the bed. I wondered if Claire was preparing to send Nanny off to a nursing home somewhere. I picked up the picture and set it on the nightstand.

Maybe I was born late or something, but I just love old photos. I don't recall ever seeing a wedding picture of Gram and her ex-husband. As matter of fact, I couldn't pick him out of a lineup. I never met the man or heard much about him. If his name ever came up, Gram instantly changed the subject.

In the photo, Dick Sr. was a handsome man. Nanny was so petite; she barely made it up to his shoulder. Her lace dress went all the way up her neck. They looked just perfect, like a couple on top of a wedding cake. She saw me smiling, and patted my hand with her good hand.

Then the premonition came. I saw the O'Neil family standing in a graveyard under trees that were full of green leaves. I knew then Nanny would be gone over the summer. I guess I made a terrible face. She squeezed my hand, and I started to cry.

"I'm sorry. It's the picture," I said, lying. "These are happy tears."

By the look she gave me, Nanny knew a load of crap when she heard it.

"I'ff had a good wife," she said. I knew she meant life instead of wife.

I sat with her until she fell asleep. Then I clipped the receiver of the baby monitor to my waistband and went downstairs to play house in the O'Neil mansion. I put some Christmas music on low and adjusted some of the swanky tree ornaments. Then I tried out every piece of furniture that I'd never dared to sit on when Claire was around. Most of it was stiff like it had just come from the showroom.

For dinner, I brought in Francis and together we ate some fancy food from the enormous refrigerator. Francis sat patient as a saint, without whining or begging and licked up all of the evidence. To my amazement, he snatched the food that I tossed him straight out of the air. We ate some brie cheese on expensive crackers. It wasn't half-bad. There were no complaints from Francis either. Looking at the crackers, I had to wonder who in their right mind would pay five dollars for such a tiny box. They didn't taste any better than cheap crackers. They just cost more.

I had barely finished cleaning up when Jason came home early, spoiling my night. The way he was just hanging around should have clued me in.

Eventually, I said, "Well, I'm off to bed." The minute I said it, he was on me like a horny hound.

"Come on, Janice. You're so hot. I think about you all the time. Just this once and I swear I'll leave you alone."

I looked into those hazel eyes of his and fell for it. I was so tired all of time. And I was tired of being alone. I let him follow me upstairs.

I also fell for it when he said, "I have a condom."

He was a lousy lay. Considering the way he kissed, I should have known better. The whole thing lasted a grueling ten minutes. The first eight minutes consisted of him slobbering all over me and pawing at me while he tried to figure out where to poke. He stabbed at me like he had a stick of dynamite he was trying to stuff up a drainpipe in the dark. I could feel his huge teeth, and he kissed with his mouth open too wide. I'm sure he kept his pants around his ankles the entire time.

When it was over, I just wanted him to get off me. I was mad at myself for being weak. I couldn't believe I had to spend the whole weekend trapped there with him. He grabbed me from behind and said, "I like staying here with you."

I fought a strong urge to vomit. "Well, Jason, you can't stay here. I'm working and I need my sleep."

"You can be such a bitch, Janice. I don't know what I ever saw in you."

"Just get out." I said.

"Whore! I've got better things to do than hang out with you."

He stormed out of the room and I heard him slam the front door and tear off in his Mustang, an early Christmas present from his parents. I went and checked on Nanny. She was still soundly sleeping. Then I locked my door, took a long, hot shower, changed the sheets, and went to sleep.

I didn't see Jason again until Sunday night when he tried being sweet again in an attempt to get into my pants for the second time. The first time had been bad enough. I told him to get lost.

"If you don't leave me alone," I said, "when your parents get home I'll tell them you raped me."

"What makes you think they'd believe some skank?" he asked.

"I've got the bruises to prove it." I said.

"Yeah, well, you asked for it."

"Is that what you tell all the girls?" I said, pissing him off.

"Fuck you, Janice!"

That was already a done deal. I never would have told Dick and Claire about what had happened. It was too mortifying, but Jason didn't know this. It wasn't far from the truth, though, to say that he'd raped me. For some reason, the threat was enough to get him to back off.

❖

When I got home on Sunday night, Mrs. S. popped her head out of her door holding Rags in her arms.

"Poor thing. You look so tired. I'll keep Mr. Raggedy Man for one more night. You look exhausted."

"Thanks Mrs. S." I said. "I am."

A few minutes later, she appeared at my door with a container in her hands. You know how everyone has a particular scent; hers was soup. Honestly, when she didn't make me dinner some nights, I'd just skip it. It was nice the way she fussed over me, bringing over stews and casseroles with things like kielbasa in them.

"You eat my special soup," she said, "and when you have time, you come and fix this electronic devil that Sheila gave me. It's beeping at me again, and it ate all my messages."

Sheila, her divorced daughter, lives in Alexandria and works for the FBI. She's always walking around with a scowl on her face. Looking into my crystal ball, I don't see a new man in her near future. Sheila has two teenage daughters. According to Mrs. S., they never visit their grandmother anymore since they're too busy fiddling around on the Internet and smooching boys.

A few nights a week, I go over to apartment fifteen to print out e-mails and download the photos sent by Sheila and her brother, Brian. Brian sends pictures of his travels with Alex, his so-called roommate. The pair of them take excellent vacations when they're not at their law practice in the district.

"Look at my boy. Isn't he the most handsome man you've ever seen? If only he could find a nice girl. I hate to think of him being all alone. It's terrible."

Brian truly is adorable and Alex has the most heavenly body I've ever seen. They helped me move some furniture once. Alex was shirtless. Imagine a Roman statue dipped in chocolate. It's a pity I'm not either of their type.

"They sure do travel to some fun places. Where was this one taken?" I asked.

"Oh, they were in Hawaii on business. Such smart boys. Brian passed the bar exam the first time he took it, you know," Mrs. S. said.

Really? I've only heard this fifty times.

"It's funny how they *always* travel together," I said.

"Well," she said. "They're good friends and business partners, dear."

I didn't want to tell Mrs. S. that Brian and Alex are more than just friends, and neither did anyone else. I just said goodnight and went to bed.

After keeping my ears open for the monitor and jumping at every sound that might have been Jason, I was a zombie come Monday morning. Stefania told me Jason had left before I got there. She might have suspected something was up, but I kept quiet, avoiding her disappointment.

Still, I desperately wanted to talk about what happened. My secret weighed on me like a lead X-ray apron. Once I got to Safe Harbor, I told Cilla the whole story. Priscilla, or Cilla for short, had taken over Rachel's job. Cilla was sweet but she couldn't keep a secret in a bucket. I don't know what I was thinking.

"What was it like? I mean, he's so gorgeous," she said with her eyes more white than brown. She'd seen Jason's picture on the society page of the newspaper. What you have to know about Cilla is that she's an incredibly nice person, even though she is somewhat sheltered. She's a year older than I am, but I'm light years ahead of her in experiences. I think she was oddly jealous. In a weird way, she wished Jason had attacked her instead of me.

"It wasn't great. I won't make the same mistake again," I swore.

"Oh, sure, I know what you mean," she said, nodding and pretending she understood. She's never actually said so, but that was when I realized that Cilla was still a virgin. I'm somewhere in the middle; not a tramp like Dee, but not a saint like Cilla.

She didn't have a clue about what I meant. Normally, talking to Cilla lifted my spirits up since she rarely had a bad day. Mel called her Miss Mary Sunshine behind her back. It was puzzling. After all the trouble Mel had with Rachel, she should have been happy to have Cilla on board. People are like that, though, never satisfied.

After talking about it, I felt worse. Then I asked a thoughtless question.

"How goes the weight loss?"

"Not great," Cilla sighed.

She'd been trying to lose twenty pounds for months, but all she did was obsess about food and then she ate even more. One time, I saw her eating leftovers from a patient's tray. It grossed me out, but I never let on that I saw her. I think she used food to try to fill up some big hole inside of her that could never get full.

Cilla looked fine, but I guess she'd been even heavier in high school and the kids had nicknamed her Priscilla the Pig. Her eyes got watery whenever she talked about it. She had so many freckles her skin looked almost pink. With her curly, strawberry-blond hair, I can see how the name stuck. Since then, she straightened and highlighted her hair, and toned down her freckles with makeup. The problem is you can't cover up the scars inside; they shine through on all of us sometimes.

CHAPTER FIVE
Facilities

Beware of false prophets, which come to you in sheep's clothing, but inwardly they are ravening wolves. —Matthew 7:15, KJV

I used to think dying of old age was the worst way to go, but now I'm thinking it's definitely malnourishment. This horrible treatment is nothing short of undignified.

Looking after people comes naturally to me. At Safe Harbor, they train the assistants to combat elderly depression by being cheerful. Sometimes, though, we're like cheerleaders for a losing team. The elderly know that they're dying. They're old, not stupid.

I like to think I make the final days of my patients more pleasant. I can't blame them for being annoyed when you insult their intelligence. They had lives. Some of them served in the war. Some owned their own businesses or came to America from another country. I like to sit and listen to them. It's an education in itself. I think what they appreciate more than anything is the knowledge their stories won't die with them.

I've had to toughen up some. I get too close to some of my patients, like Mrs. Benjamin. One day, she'd been on my mind all morning. Whenever I tried to think about something else, I'd see her face. During my lunch rounds, I switched her with one of my sleeping patients.

"I hope you're hungry, Mrs. B! I've got hot stuff coming through."

It was our little joke. She'd told me that when she was my age she'd been hot stuff, just like me.

I carefully laid the tray down on the table next to her single bed. The news was on her TV, and they were going on about an elevated terrorist threat in the Washington DC area.

"I'll bet you're glad we live here and not there, huh, Mrs. B.?" I said.

She didn't answer.

"It's meatloaf, your favorite," I went on mustering as much cheer as possible.

"Not today, dear," she said. "George is taking me home. I can eat when I get there."

"Mrs. B.," I said. "George passed two years ago now. He'd want you to eat something to keep up your strength."

"How can that be, Janice? He's standing right there next to you," she said pointing to the blank space beside me.

I got a woeful case of the shivers, and I started looking around. I didn't see anybody, but she sure did. Next thing, she left our conversation for an entirely new one.

"Yes, I'm ready, George. I'll just get my purse."

That was the last thing she said before her body quit with one quick shiver and an uneasy stillness. I ran over and opened the window. One of the evening shift nurses told me once that a fresh spirit might become stuck if you didn't give it a way to escape.

I was still crying and standing by the window when Mel came in. She called the attendants to tend to Mrs. Benjamin. Then she put her arm around my shoulder and led me out to the break room.

❖

The worst part of my job is dealing with the families who never come around. Then they show up later to collect on the insurance policy or fight over the meager inheritance. I'm growing what Gram called a rhinoceros hide. Still, sometimes I'd like to scream in the faces of the delinquent relatives, "Where the hell have you been?"

I don't say anything, though. I'd lose my job. Then where would I be? I'd be out on my tail—that's where. I don't ever want to get old.

Of course, I might not have to worry about that. I'm imagining all of the awful things that happen to people in captivity. I'm thinking anything these bastards have planned; I've surely already been through worse.

❖

English is back. He doesn't say anything. He just brings me to use what he calls the *facilities*.

Once I'm inside, I pee right quick and then fly to the window to see what's out there. On the left side of the window, close to the toilet, I noticed a gap in the paper covering. I peek through it to see if it's day or night. It's neither. It's either dusk or dawn. To keep track of the days, I'd planned on counting daylight. Now I'm not sure. I hurry up and wash my hands.

He's back already and knocking at the door. As he takes me back to my dank little room, I hear music and smell chicken and garlic. I wonder how long it takes before your stomach begins to eat its own lining. He comes into the closet with me. He turns on the light and guides me over to the bed. Across from me, I hear the legs of a chair scraping across the wooded floor. It creaks as he settles in. Our knees touch at first, so he adjusts his chair backward.

"What's with this music?" I ask.

"Beethoven. Do you like classical music?"

"I've never thought about it."

"Shocking."

His condescending tone pisses me off. "It's not the same group you were playing the other day."

"No. I was playing Brahms."

"Like the lullaby?" I ask him.

"Yes, but not that one."

I remember hearing someone playing a piano along with the music. I take a chance and ask, "How long have you been playing the piano?" He doesn't answer right away.

"All of my life," he says trying to disguise the surprise in his voice.

With my hands still tied, he has to feed me. The food is spicy. I've always wanted to try exotic food. I guess you can find good in any circumstance. He doesn't work in health care. I know because he doesn't wait long enough between bites. Not to risk making him mad, I chew faster. When the food hits my hollow gut, it makes a gurgling sound. Maybe if I tried being nice we could get along.

"So, what's your name?" I casually ask.

"My name is of no concern to you."

It was worth a try. He presses the fork to my mouth, and I open it like a baby bird. Food is safe territory. With my mouth full, I ask, "Whas this called?"

"Shawarma." His hand touches my face by accident. I jump but quickly settle back down. When I swallow, spices cling to my tongue, tingling, sweet, and sour.

"It's good," I say.

"Thank you. That's enough chitchat, Janice. How did you know about the tunnel?"

I'm feeling groggy now. I'm not sure if it's the music or the meal. Confused I say, "I don't know what you're talking about."

With a clink, the fork is back on the plate and my stomach groans disappointment at my big mouth.

"Janice, what did I tell you? What do you think happens when I lose tolerance?"

He takes my hands. With his warm, smooth hands caressing mine he says, "These hands have killed. What is one more useless female?"

I lose my breath for a moment. "Here's the thing…"

"Yes?"

I draw a total blank. It sounds crazy every time I explain it.

Hello? Voices in my head, do you remember me? It's Janice. I could sure use some help down here!

What comes to mind is that God helps those who help themselves.

Is this supposed to be some kind of joke? Very funny! I'm up Crap Creek without a paddle, and my mind is playing tricks.

"Perhaps your brain lacks nourishment," English says slowly. "I apologize for your poor treatment. The others neglect your needs when I'm not here." He slides a forkful of chicken into my mouth.

I swallow. For the first time since this began, I feel hopeful. If I cooperate, he might let me go. He wants answers. I don't really know anything. It's all just a big misunderstanding. Once I explain the premonitions to him, he'll have no reason to keep me any longer.

"Take your time. What is time, anyway? Do you know it took us six months to plan the attack on the tunnel, and it took you only a few seconds to spoil it?"

Then again, he'll have no reason to keep me alive either.

"Well," I say. "I see things before they happen—futuristic things."

"Liar!" I hear a tingling, clunking sound as metal hits the wood floor. His voice has changed. He's moving again. He's standing over me now, tapping on my head with his finger.

"Think hard, Janice! Someone told you something. Who was it? Just give me his name." He leans in closely, his hot breath flooding my face. "Is it one name or are there two traitors?"

I'm baffled. I seriously don't know what to say. If I say that God speaks to me, this surely won't sit well. I start talking faster but not making any more sense.

"I really can see things before they happen. I see them in my head. It's like I'm watching a movie. Sometimes I see things that have already happened. Sometimes I see people and I just know they're heading for trouble. When we drove through the tunnel, I saw all of these faces. They were flying at me in my mind and I couldn't breathe. I knew they were going to die."

"Valkillibah!" With a loud bang, the chair hits the floor. "Muhammad!"

At first, I think English is praying. Then someone else comes in. The newcomer doesn't smell like Ape; he smells like incense. My body is wide-awake with adrenaline, but my mind is still fuzzy. They argue and call me *Za-hera* and *Mooshau-wetha*. They say these words the same way English says *American*.

The second man leaves. I hear him yelling outside of the room, but with breaks in-between. He's on the telephone. English paces around, muttering and huffing. This isn't what he expected. He stops moving and exhales slowly. "Janice, let's start again. Be honest this time, yes?"

"I know it sounds crazy—believe me, I know. The truth is the truth, though, whether you believe me or not. If you don't…well… then you should just kill me. Go ahead and get it over with."

"Do you think I will let you get away so easily?" English asks. "I have something more painful in mind."

Shit. Think fast, Janice. Think fast. "Don't you want to know if there are any messages for you first—I mean, before you hurt me." I can't tell you where I come up with the nerve, hoping my plan will save my skin.

"What messages? You mean delusions or sorcery."

Where in the hell are the voices when I need them most? I haven't heard from a soul. I'm betting on a losing hand here.

The other man is back and seems to be giving English instructions. I'll call him Chief. English translates some of what he says. "My brother thinks women and infidels are like sheep. A skinny, poor American girl could never be a prophet—only a witch or a sorceress."

"OK. Then how did I know about your plan? I'm nothing special, you just said it yourself."

He doesn't answer. A bead of sweat slips down and settles in the gap of my bra. I'm shaking. I have the chills all over. Usually chills mean a premonition is coming. Please make it be so.

I smell something awful. It takes me a minute to realize the smell is coming from me. My own body betrays me again. Fear is the nasty odor of my sweat. I keep trying and say to English, "Something brought us together. Don't you see that?"

"I see before me an animal. A fox that I tracked and caught," he says.

Suddenly, I remember his face when he was asking for directions. He has warm eyes, almond-shaped eye, like mine. His skin is tan, but not a summer tan. I noticed his dark curly hair and thought, "He's good-looking, but he's not from around here."

Then a grainy black-and-white film plays in my mind. I see a dusty place, an explosion, and men running. One man bends over another man's body. I see smoke, fire, debris. I see English with fury in his dark eyes.

I tell him, "This isn't the first plan you've had that's backfired. You lost someone—someone close to you—in an explosion." I hear the other man gasp. He mutters something to English, who snaps something back, his voice low and slow. The door opens and closes and then I'm alone again with English.

"I'm not so easily fooled by your sorcery. You will have to do better to convince me, Janice."

"Suit yourself. But if it was up to me, I'd want to know what's coming next."

I'm instantly uncomfortable. He leans in close, invading my space. I sense his face pass in front of mine. His scruff scratches my check. With his hot breath in my ear, he says, "But I already know what's coming next. If you were what you say you are, you would be terrified. Do you think I'm playing with you, little girl? I only play games when I know I will win. You are making a fool's bet by gambling with your life. Be warned. You have underestimated your opponent."

He stands up again and wraps his hands around my head, holding it like a ball. He turns my face upward.

"Unlike you, I have nothing to lose. These are dangerous odds for you. Start confessing your sins, Catholic girl." He tosses my head back and slams the door with such force I'm still shaking when the lock clicks into place.

CHAPTER SIX
Madonna

I either just bought myself more time or have precious little left to find a way out of this. I'm missing a connection here. How did English know that I knew something about the tunnel? I didn't tell anyone but Stefania. Who would she tell? I mean, she is a foreigner. I know I'm being a bad friend by letting my mind go there. These men aren't Italian. They're Arabs or something.

I also told Cilla. Crap. Gram used to say, "A secret's only safe between two people if one of them is dead." Well, this is about to be true. Who in the hell could Cilla have told?

More importantly, what do I tell English when he comes back? I'm not afraid to die. I've looked death square in the face plenty of times. I'll keep on telling the truth. It's that simple. Unless the truth isn't what he wants to hear.

If I die, what happens to Jessie? Could the sisters legally keep her? She'd be better off without me. I've failed her as mother. Look at me. I'm as bad as Dee—worse, even. Whenever there's a fork in the road, I choose the wrong path every freaking time.

The fork. I feel around on the floor with my fingers. Damn blindfold. There. Nope. No matter. Even without the blindfold, it's a cave in here. Resorting to instinct, I drop down on all fours, searching around with my hands. I've got it. I press my thumb on the sharp, pointy end. A fork can be a fine weapon.

I slip it between the mattress and the box spring. Since English is so mad, I hope he'll forget he dropped it. If he finds out I've stashed it, though, things will take a bad turn. I risk it and leave the fork under the mattress for now. They can't keep me here. If need be, I'm prepared to stab English with the fork. I have no flipping idea what I'll do after that, but I'm not going down easy.

Seeing English in that dusty field was the first premonition I've had here. Why haven't there been more? Is it because I let doubt snake into my mind? I let fear shake my faith.

People talk about blind faith, but faith is never blind. Those who have faith see more than the rest. The faithful know you can't use your eyes to see faith; it comes before knowledge, before proof. By asking for signs, you only prove yourself a nonbeliever. For believers, the signs are visible all around. I let myself forget faith is the magic key and I stopped praying. I've been more worried about saving my skinny behind, about my earthly self. Janice, you dumb ass.

I start with the Lord's Prayer, an act of contrition, and a Hail Mary. Mary was a mother. She'd understand what I'm going through. According to the bible, Mary had sought shelter when Christmas was coming. Christmas is only a few weeks away. I refuse to miss Jessie's first Christmas. I so wanted it to be like last year, but minus some of the drama.

❖

The Saturday before last Christmas, I was still plodding along in ignorant bliss. For once, I had some extra cash in my pocket. I'd seen a store near the mall in Annapolis that sold religious statues and things. I went in there to buy something Gram could add to her chapel collection.

For a tiny place, it was stacked high with paintings and statues of Jesus, Mary, and the gang. I scanned the bookshelves. There were bibles, prayer books, and religious self-help books. There was even one book called, *How to Talk to God*. What would make anyone think he was an authority on that subject?

In the children's corner, there were picture books, puzzles, stuffed animals and Noah's Ark play sets. The toys were arranged around a miniature table and some chairs on top of a rainbow rug. *Leave it to the Holy Rollers to get them while they're young.* There were some nice things, though. I thought it was pity I didn't know anyone with kids.

As I strolled up the aisles, the sales clerk pinned her piercing blue eyes to my back. She was around Dee's age, mid-thirties maybe, with frizzy red hair and freckles. I guess the way I checked the prices on everything looked suspicious or maybe I wasn't her typical customer.

I found an affordable statue of the Madonna cradling the baby Jesus and carried it around with me. I looked up and smiled at the clerk. I'm friendly by nature and I didn't want her assuming I was a thief. She smiled back creating some softness on her skeletal face.

At the jewelry tower near the register, I picked out two Saint Agatha medals—one for me, and one for Cilla. I'd been reading to Nanny about Saint Agatha, the patron saint of nurses. At Safe Harbor, Cilla and me needed all of the help we could get. As I put my items to purchase on the counter, the clerk reached over and touched my arm saying, "A baby girl is a special blessing."

"What?" I think my jaw actually hung open for several minutes.

"Your baby," she said. "They want you to know that you needn't worry. You'll both be just fine."

"No offense, lady, but I don't know what the heck you're talking about," I said. "I'm just here to buy a statue for my grandmother. So, that's what I'm doing." I grabbed the pendants and the statue and pushed them across the counter, as if they'd somehow protect me from her brand of crazy.

"I'm terribly sorry," the woman said. "I shouldn't have said anything. I rarely approach people unless they send off a certain vibe. You seemed particularly receptive." Her face colored as red as her hair. She didn't say anything else while she rang up my items and wrapped the statue in tissue paper. At the last minute, I saw her slip something into the bag.

"It's OK," I said. "I get that all the time. I must have one of those faces."

It's true. I've always been a weirdo magnet. People constantly tell me their life stories, whether or not I want to hear them. I made a note right then to try to appear less open. I had enough problems.

"Just the same, you have my apologies," she said.

"No worries," I said. "Thanks."

"Thank you and enjoy the rest of your day," she smiled as I left.

Outside of the store, I peered into the bag. *You seem particularly whacked out. Vibe my butt.* She'd put a business card in with my purchases. It read, "Annie Kellogg: Psychic Healer, Spiritual Readings and Reiki Massage." The card listed an e-mail address and a telephone number.

Then it hit me like a sucker punch square to the face. *A baby girl? Cazzo!* She thought I was pregnant. So help me, if that weasel Jason had gotten me pregnant. For a moment, I had some homicidal thoughts about him. I mean I was no virgin when we met, but I'd managed to reach twenty-years-old childless. This was all I flipping needed.

I couldn't think straight. I stood in the middle of the parking lot unsure of which way to turn. Everywhere I looked, I saw people wallowing in Christmas spirit. It was like a Bing Crosby song. Happy couples were shopping and holding hands. Angelic children peered into store windows. Carols blasted from the loudspeakers. I had to get the heck out of there.

Normally I did my shopping late at night. I'd go to stores that were open for twenty-four hours, the kind of places where the drunks and the kooks talked to themselves. Them, I could handle.

This is what happens when you start thinking your life can turn around and you might have a chance to make something of your sorry self. I actually stopped breathing for a minute before I sprinted to my car. I drove to the nearest pharmacy, grabbed a pregnancy test, and paid for it as quickly as humanly possible.

On the way home, I passed a gas station and thought about stopping to use the bathroom to take the test. Then I changed my mind. Who would want to hold onto that memory for the rest of her life? It would have been like a marriage proposal in a cemetery.

I sped home like an intoxicated maniac, unable to remember how I'd gotten back to my apartment. Right quick, I peed on the stick. Sure enough, the effing thing had a big old plus sign on it. Just to be sure, I repeated the whole process with the second stick and got the same darn result. *Fuck.* It was all I could say. Gram always said swearing was a sign of a low-class nature. I couldn't help it though. Once again, I'd proven I was just that.

Really God? What else can happen?

I never should have asked this question.

Calming down somewhat, I decided not to think about my pregnancy or mention it to anyone until after the New Year. As if ignoring it would make it go away. I didn't want to ruin Christmas for Gram, even if I'd already wrecked my own. What were a few more weeks? If I hadn't taken the test, I technically wouldn't even know I was pregnant. Right? Time could have gone by, and I would have been none the wiser. Why had I been in such a rush to take the test? I've never been a good test taker. Here was another big old F.

It took all my willpower not to tell Cilla. After the first week, though, it got easier. She never would have kept it to herself. I guess I should have considered this more before I told her about my premonitions. I imagined if she shared my psychic secret with anyone else they would just think she was nuts. Me knocked up they all would have believed and I wasn't ready for the whole world to know.

To figure out how far gone I was, I started counting out the days. It was just a few weeks by my calculation. Enough time to decide what to do. No one was likely to notice I seemed different. They'd all be too wrapped up with Christmas.

CHAPTER SEVEN
Insidious

Call now, if there be any that will answer thee; and to which of the saints wilt thou turn? —Job 5:1, KJV

It feels like a long time since English last came to my room. My throat might actually seal itself shut from the dryness. I start thinking about all of the different ways there are to die. How long can you live without water? A few days? I try to conjure up some spit in my mouth, but there isn't any.

Instead of the music, the TV is on. Someone's watching game shows. I hear him laughing. It's not English. It sounds like the voice from the first night and different from Chief's voice. That means Ape is on guard duty alone. Ape is the one English calls Saif. When you can't see, your other senses take up the slack.

Where does English go when he leaves? Is anyone looking for me? Is Jessie all right? Does she think I've left her? She's only three months old. Is she old enough to know something has happened to me? Is she aware enough to miss me? In my mind, I conjure her image sleeping like an angel while I rock her in my arms.

I'm sure I missed Thanksgiving by now. I'd planned to make Christmas cookies with Mrs. S. on the day after Thanksgiving. They would have been Jessie's first Christmas cookies.

Before Christmas last year, my spirit was in the toilet. I was hiding my pregnancy and sick all of time. Outside my apartment door, Mrs. S. had left a tin with a note stuck on it that said:

Dear Janice,
Here's a little something to help fatten you up. I'll be at Sheila's with Brian and Alex if you need anything. Merry Christmas!
Love,
Anne Sirkulanitz

I opened the lid and breathed in sugar and vanilla. The cookies were frosted and shaped like little bells and wreaths. There were some gingerbread men with cute frosting clothes. I don't care for gingerbread, so I pretended each one of those little men was Jason. I bit their heads off and spit them out one by one. It was a darn shame they didn't have tiny little penises.

On Christmas Day, Gram and I planned to go to Mass together just like we did every Sunday. Nonetheless, I felt guilty about my new plans for Christmas Eve. I was spending the evening at the *festa* with the Fortini family. I needed to tell Gram about it in person.

You wouldn't know it was Christmas by looking at Gram's place. She always decorated her cottage with religious items. The only addition was the nativity scene in the living room. Ever since I was eight years old, it had been my job to set it up. The tattered box was waiting for me.

"You look pale and thin Janice. Are you eating enough?" Gram asked, studying me. Looking tired was something we had in common. Her skin was as gray as her cropped hair, which was in desperate need of a new style.

"Yes I might be a bit tired. I'm still working two jobs," I said, hiding the fact that I was also a smidgen pregnant.

"I'll make you a sandwich," Gram said. "I have some nice olive loaf."

My stomach lurched at the sound of it. "No thanks. I had some leftover soup before I came over."

The cottage decor hadn't changed since my great-grandmother had owned the place, worn by the years, like its owner. I dropped my purse onto the small, rickety kitchen table. I reached into the avocado refrigerator for a can of generic soda. After a few slugs, I carried the can into the living room and walked across the rope rug; its rainbow colors had long since faded. Settling into the armchair, I avoided the hole where the stuffing poked out and tickled you. The nativity scene box lay on the seat below the bay window. When Gram came in with her sandwich, I let her have the chair and sat on the floor by the window where I began my work.

Gram considered vanity to be a sin, along with frivolous spending. I noticed she was still wearing work clothes—her tan, polyester, elastic-waist pants and her white polyester blouse. She rotated through the same few outfits. Whenever I bought her anything new, she returned it and found some way to give the money back to me.

"This year, I thought I might mix it up," I said. "Maybe I could put Joseph on the left and Mary on the right. Some of the animals could peek in the window of the stable to check things out."

Gram finished chewing a bite of her sandwich and swallowed. "With some things, Janice, tradition is always best."

How did I know she would say this? I knelt in front of the wooden stable and arranged the plaster of Paris figurines from memory. It was my job, but Gram always supervised me.

"Janice, the donkey is too close to the sheep. He needs to move back. The angel should be on the peak of the roof. It's the highest point. Mary needs to look down into the cradle."

"How's that?" I said, turning Mary's small kneeling figurine. I wondered whether Mary felt frightened or only excited about what was to come.

"Yes," Gram said. "That's better, Dee—I mean Janice. I don't know why I do that sometimes."

Seriously? I do.

"It's okay," I said as I picked up baby Jesus, so tiny and weightless. I held him for a moment before tucking him into a piece of cotton and slipping him behind the stable. It didn't seem right that he was all alone back there, but it was tradition. Jesus never made his appearance in the cradle until the stroke of midnight on Christmas Eve.

"Gram, I thought that maybe I'd get you a tree. Remember how we always used to have one when I lived here with you?"

"Don't be silly, Janice," Gram said. "It's nothing but a big waste of money and you need every red cent."

"Sure, I understand. By the way, I'm going to Christmas Eve at my friend Stefania's parent's house. They said you're more than welcome to come along."

"Oh, Janice you know I don't like people fussing over me. There's too much to do at the church anyway. Who would take care of all of the preparations? You go ahead. Enjoy yourself."

I'm sure she never intended to make me feel bad for having occasional fun. It was just her way. I wondered what she would say when I told her about the secret that was growing heavier inside of me every day.

❖

That night, I lay in my bed and agonized over my life. A thought crept into my mind, an insidious thought. It was like an old boyfriend who slips in through the backdoor unwelcome, still you don't object.

What if I decided not to have the baby?

The only person who knew about my baby was the psychic woman. I would probably never see her again. I had enough money saved up, and everything in my life would go back to normal.

Then the vision came. Jesus was standing on top of a mountain with his arms stretched out and his white robes flowing. In his serenity, I felt the enormous weight of sorrow. Then the mountain changed and shapes appeared where the land had been—shapes with infant faces. There were so many I couldn't count them all. Their tiny bodies overlapped. White wings fluttered at their sides. They smiled at me, these angel babies, a million smiles at once.

I ran to the restroom, revisited by the soup I had eaten for dinner.

❖

On Christmas Eve, I had the day off from my first job. Relatives were visiting the O'Neil family for the holidays. After the rough night I'd had, it felt like heaven to sleep in. I also needed to get some rest before I underwent the torture of the Christmas party at Safe Harbor. All of the residents who didn't have plans to go home to their families would be stuck there with us for their sole entertainment.

Under bright fluorescent lights, Cilla hung fireproof garland around the common room. To cover up the stale antiseptic odor, I sprayed air freshener that smelled like pine trees. The artificial tree we had set up lurched to one side. No matter how many times we tried to right it, it was still wrong. Then we ran out of time.

The residents came in. Some staggered in on walkers with tennis balls stuck to the front legs. Others slumped over in their wheelchairs were rolled in with the help of the other assistants. All of us on staff danced around the residents singing *Rudolf the Red-Nosed Reindeer* and knowing all the while that the sweets and rich foods we fed them were sure to give them the runs later.

I wanted to run screaming from the room. Considering I had the most seniority, I wondered why I hadn't taken the day off. Even dumber, I'd volunteered for the late shift on Christmas Day. I was there because the others had children and families. I needed the money more than ever, especially since if Mel learned about my secret, she might fire my dumb ass. I guess in truth I needed my head examined.

As if Mel could read my mind, before my shift ended, she called me into her office. I nearly passed a brick. Thoughts raced through my head. I assumed Cilla had blabbed or Jason had flapped his gums about our one passionless night. With a mug of eggnog in my hand, I walked into Mel's office. She was perched on the edge of her desk. If you looked carefully at Mel, you could see beauty hiding underneath her hard mask of sorrow.

"Take a load off, Janice. You've been working your tail off."

I settled into one of two chairs that were facing her. It felt weird to sit down without being behind a steering wheel. She spiked my eggnog with a shot from her secret stash. I know I shouldn't have been drinking, but I couldn't let her get suspicious.

"Thanks, Mel. Merry Christmas." After Gram, Mel was the second person I most dreaded confessing to about my pregnancy. Pretending to sip my drink, I considered blurting it out. Instead, I looked down at the thick, yellow liquid in my cup. I watched a speck of nutmeg float like an ant across the surface. The eggnog's new boozy odor made my stomach roll. I set the cup down on her desk and asked, "So, what are your holiday plans, Mel? Are you seeing family and friends?"

"Oh, something along those lines," she said. Mel's private life was the biggest mystery at Safe Harbor. She was an expert at changing the subject.

"Say, listen, Janice, you're doing a hell of a job over at the O'Neil house. Dick is crazy about you. He wanted you to have this."

She snatched an envelope off the desk and handed it to me. I peered into it at the small pile of cash. "Wow. Thanks." *Merry guilty Christmas.*

If Mel had been a different kind of boss, she would have kept the money and I'd have been none the wiser.

"Consider it a holiday bonus." She said and poured herself another drink that was more whisky than eggnog. I thanked her, tucked the money in the front pocket of my scrubs, and headed out. I felt sure Mel planned to spend another night with her buddy, Jack Daniels. Even though she never appeared drunk, I always knew she had a problem. I couldn't blame her, though, running Safe Harbor would have driven anybody to the bottle.

The meeting with Mel had put me off schedule. After I punched out, I did a lightening change in the women's room, cleaning up as best I could. From what I could see, nothing in my face gave me away. My hair was a feral mane that no amount of water would smooth, but fresh eyeliner and lip-gloss brought me back from the dead. I brushed my teeth three times to get the eggnog taste out of my mouth. I wondered if there were really eggs in it. It sounded disgusting. I imagined the little egg growing inside of me—a tiny, secret egg that had hatched unbeknownst to me and was coming to life. I felt ill.

I would have cancelled my plans if Stefania hadn't made me promise I'd come, luring me with menu descriptions until my stomach agreed for me.

"I can't wait for you to meet my family," Stefania said. "Everybody's coming to get fatter on the famous Fortini food."

"No wonder you're such a great cook. It runs in the family."

"No, no. All Italian women know how to cook. I used to work every day at *Basilico*, but the O'Neil's pay better and I can make all the recipes I want instead of the same old things. Besides, they give me room and board. My family doesn't understand."

"Why? You have a great job."

"Because, Janeeze, they want me to live at home until I'm married. Can you imagine? One day, I say to Mama, 'What if I don't ever get married?' She clutches her chest. 'What are you talking about? Of course, you'll get married.' She said it like I was *pazzo*. She wants to send me to Napoli this summer. She thinks I don't know what she's up to."

"What is she up to?" I asked.

"I'm to stay with my Aunt Elena, the matchmaker."

"They can't force you to get married. It's not the dark ages." I said.

"You don't know, Janeeze, the shame of being unmarried at my age."

Stefania was so well put together I never could figure out exactly how old she was. I guessed she wasn't much older than me or Bridge, maybe in her early twenties but hardly an Old Maid.

"If you were running *Basilico* would they still think you needed a husband?"

"Of course. But they would never give me *Basilico*. They want Francesco, my younger brother, to take over. That's why I took this job. What's the point? It makes me so angry. How can I explain Francesco? He is a playboy and so lazy. He doesn't care about anything or anybody but his, you know, his fun. Half the time, he doesn't even show up at work. Yet he can do no wrong. I want to be my own boss, to have a business all my own. So, I save my money. Maybe I can cater big parties, who knows?"

"It's a great idea. I envy you Stefania, how you know what you want."

CHAPTER EIGHT
Il Cenacolo

In my little Honda Civic, it was cold enough for me to see my breath. The heat finally groaned on when I crossed the Bay Bridge and was nearly there. Snow flew at my windshield, as if the angels in heaven had all decided to shake out their rugs at once. Flurries blurred the streetlights, replacing the stars with swirls against the ink-black sky.

I found the neighborhood. Passing elegant houses with their shrubs trimmed in strings of lights, white and colored, glowing polka dots under a snow-sheet. I circled the car-lined street twice. Six houses down from the Fortini family home, I parked my beater, which had more rust than paint, between a Cadillac and a Mercedes. It looked like a homeless guy on a bus full of businessmen.

When the snow sputtered to a stop, the air took a wicked turn, stinging my nostrils and coming out in puffs. With fish shaped lips, I made smoke rings of the frigid air and suddenly missed the real thing. A cigarette would have calmed my nerves.

I missed having a warm coat more. I hugged my arms across my chest, hearing Gram's voice in my head saying, "Janice, why don't you ever wear your winter coat? You'll wind up with pneumonia."

"Cold doesn't make you sick Gram," I imagined myself saying. "Germs do."

"That's nonsense, Janice," she'd say.

On my walk up to their red brick house, a nervous twist twirled in my belly, a mixture of doubt and fear. I thought to myself, "What am I doing here?"

White lights coiled around the columns of the house. Evergreen wreaths with golden ribbons and balls hung from eight windows across the front. It was all a pleasant distraction from freezing to death.

I scampered the rest of the way to the door, pushing the bell hard with my raw, red finger. On the front steps, something caught my eye under the lights. It was a clump of snow shaped like a perfect Y. I looked up to try to find the tree limb that had dropped this sign. There was none. I just saw the gutter. What did this mean? Was it a question? Was it an answer? Like a yes, but to what question?

No answer came when I rang the doorbell a second time. The crowd noise and beams of light leaked from the house. I pressed the buzzer a third time, shivering and hoping I was at the right house. I compared the address in my head to the house numbers on the brick siding. Then the door swung open. Warm air escaped, along with the commotion that was coming from inside. A slim, tan-skinned man in his twenties held the door open. He moved his eyes over me.

"Hi. I'm…" I said, forgetting my own name for a second. "Janice."

With chocolate eyes, he smiled so warmly, I melted.

"Janeeze. Steffi's girlfriend. Come in. Come in. We're all waiting for you."

He moved aside and motioned me in. I was hoping that the forty-degree temperature shift inside wouldn't make my nose run. As I passed him, he took my shoulders and pulled me into him, kissing my cheeks one at a time. His lips felt soft and warm on my frozen skin.

"*Buon Natale.*"

"Buona…" I said. "Yeah, what you said."

"Oh, you're like gelato," he laughed and rubbed his hands up and down my arms. "I'll tell Steffi you're here." His cologne filled the gap in the air between us. Breathing in, I could taste it, sweet and poisonous at the same time. Thoughts whirled through my brain, but no words formed in my mouth before he disappeared into the crowd.

Overheated and lost in a loud human sea, I searched for him and for Stefania. People smiled at me. They said, "Auguri" and "Buon Natale." I smiled back flummoxed, until Stefania found my arm and linked our elbows.

"I was worried. I thought you changed your mind," she said, moving me through the crowd. She stopped at one point and asked an elderly man, "*Dove Mama*?"

"*In cucina*," he said, waving toward the kitchen. Then he turned to me and sandwiched my hand between his small, thin hands. "Hello, I am Vincenzo Fortini. I am Stefania's father. You must be the lovely Janice."

"It's very nice to meet you," was all I had time to say before Stefania tugged me away and weaved a path toward the kitchen. Food smells spiraled around me: garlic, fried fish, and tomato sauce. I looked down at my stomach, pitched inward and concave. I might have drooled just a little. Stefania pushed the kitchen door open and, dragged me inside with her.

The kitchen was a secret oasis, restaurant sized and filled with women chopping, rolling, mixing, and frying things. At a long wooden farm table, a middle-aged woman slowly arranged meat and olives on a huge salad. At the stove on the far side of the room, Mrs. Fortini stirred a concoction in a pot, which looked like it could hold a large animal. Above her head, steam wafted up into a fan big enough to suck up a small child. Stefania prattled in Italian to some of the women. Then brought me over to her mother and said, "Mama, this is my friend Janeeze."

Mrs. Fortini stopped stirring, turned and wiped her hands on her sauce-stained apron. She took my face in her flour-covered hands and kissed me. Then she squeezed me so tight I feared I might lose consciousness. It was like hugging a giant pillow.

"Steffi has told me so much about you! Welcome. *Auguri*!"

"It's very nice to meet you," I said. "You have a beautiful home." I learned from Gram that it was standard practice to compliment your Hostess. I was being honest with Mrs. Fortini, but it still sounded robotic coming from me. Stefania abandoned me to go chop tomatoes. The pot started to boil and Mrs. Fortini went back to stirring. I stood watching everyone, my body slowly defrosting.

Beneath weight and years, I could see Stefania in her mother's face. Mrs. Fortini tucked wet ringlets back into the bun of her gray-streaked hair exposing damp rings under the arms of her blouse. I could imagine Stefania in years to come, her cute figure vanishing and big cankles forming where her tiny ankles once were. I think they forgot I was there until I offered to help. With the sauce under control, Mrs. Fortini turned to me again.

"We're so happy you could join us tonight. Please, Janey, make yourself at home. Back to cooking for me or we'll never eat tonight. Steffi, I need your help with the calamari." Stefania shooed me out of the kitchen to go relax and enjoy myself.

I was adrift again in the living room. I did my best to mingle while I searched for *him,* the boy with the chocolate eyes who had opened the door for me earlier. The house was as grand as the O'Neil mansion but different in every way. This house welcomed visitors with cozy couches and chairs, not stiff and showy furniture. Family pictures covered the walls. Patches of bright wallpaper peeked out underneath them. The worn rugs and statues reminded me of an antique store minus the price tags. Over the fireplace, I stared up at a painting that I knew well: *Il Cenacolo* or *The Last Supper*.

I meandered until exhaustion dragged me down into a vacant armchair. Resting, I admired the Christmas tree, sparkling brighter than the Chesapeake Bay at sunrise. I fixed my gaze on the silver sequined star on top that sparkled so regally. I closed my eyes and wished for guidance in my wayward life.

Some of Stefania's relatives stopped to talk to me, but I was having a hard time remembering who was who. So many family members shared the same first name. There were four Tonys, three Vinnys, and I can't tell you how many Marias. It didn't help that they all looked similar. I memorized associations, to remember Aunt Maria with the glasses and Uncle Vinnie with the mole near his left eye.

The aunts had either short black hair or long hair pinned up. Stefania's multiple female cousins all seemed to be falling out of their low-cut sweaters, blouses, and tight, glittery dresses. I wondered how many hours it had taken them to tease up their silky, black hairdos. They wore more makeup and jewelry at one time than I did in a solid year. I felt completely unfeminine in their presence.

I looked down at my jeans, my boots, and my festive red Kmart sweater. When no one was looking, I gave myself a whiff to see if I emitted that icky hospital smell. Yuck. Hair holds tight to the smell of chemical cleaners and smoke. The perfumed crowd and the heavenly scents of the kitchen worked hard to cover any odor I might have had.

Stefania must have told her family we were good friends. Everyone I met grabbed me and kissed both of my cheeks. The second Aunt Maria, but without glasses, took my hands with her icy fingers and called me *bella*. Unaccustomed to affectionate strangers, I wasn't sure what to do. I just kept smiling.

The men either had big, round bellies or were like walking bags of bones. Some were balding or had thick, bushy eyebrows, and weathered faces. Everyone was different, but somehow they all looked like a matching set.

I listened to Vincenzo telling a long story with his hands to a group of men. "*Senti, Vincenzo,*" a slim man with jet-black eyes and charcoal hair interrupted. Dressed in black from head to toe,

I guessed he was around my age. He said, "*Prego*. I'll tell the story the way it really happened." All of the men laughed but I didn't get his joke.

"Maximus the great story teller, no one wants to hear your fairy tales. What do you know about it?" Vincenzo said, making the others laugh again.

I had just about given up looking for the chocolate-eyed man when he appeared with twin wingmen and those eyes of his fixed on me. He called Maximus over and introduced me to his crew. "Janeeze, did you meet everyone?"

"I'm not sure." I said.

"My sister is worried. She asked me to check on you." So this was Francesco. I should have guessed.

"This is Ciro, Enzo, and Max. They are my cousins."

As the only blonde-haired woman, I was an instant celebrity surrounded by four sizzling Italians who all wanted tell stories about the others. I swam in a dizzy mixture of cologne and machismo and floated on a swell of laughter. Francesco took my hands and locked his eyes with mine. I heard myself sigh loudly at the way my name rolled off his tongue.

"Janeeze is here all alone. Can you guys believe it?" Francesco said.

I'm not alone.

"What? Where is your boyfriend?" Enzo asked. "He must be crazy. He lets you go out alone when you're so beautiful."

"I'm between boyfriends at the moment," I confessed.

"Unbelievable!" Ciro added throwing his hands into the air.

"Janeeze, what are you doing on New Year's? We'll all of us take you out," Francesco said.

"Oh, I'm sure I'll have to work," I groaned.

"Work? No, no, no work. Americans are always working and never having fun!" Francesco shook his head as if the gesture could make work disappear. I believed he could make anything happen. "Italians work only to live. Living is about pleasure," he explained.

I know now that God has a sense of humor. Like a diabetic in a candy store, the irony of my situation wasn't lost on little old pregnant me. I would have taken any one of them but if they knew I was about to become a mother would any of them have taken me?

Stefania rescued me before I could do myself or anyone else any more harm. "Leave her alone you animals," she said to the group.

"What makes you think she wants to be alone?" Francesco asked.

Mrs. Fortini popped out of the kitchen with a tray of food in her hands.

"*Piacere a tutti andare,*" she said. "Everyone, please come to the dining room."

"Your mom must be so tired. She's been going all night," I said to Stefania.

"No! She loves this. She wants to take care of everybody. Please! She lives for this."

The dining room was set restaurant style with one fantastically long table down the middle of the room. Sandwiched between Stefania and Francesco, I swallowed up conversation as plentiful as the food. Platter after platter came through the swinging kitchen door—trays of cheese, cold cuts, fried squid, shrimp, meatballs, eggplant, lasagna, chicken in lemon sauce, and pasta with tomato sauce or *ragu*, as they called it, which was nothing like the jarred kind I used.

Since the relatives who didn't speak English made the others translate in order to talk to me, I learned enough Italian to fill my monthly quota. Every time I said something correctly, they'd all shout, "*Brava!*"

Toward the end of the night, I was well past my bursting point. Aunt Maria with the glasses popped a piece of marinated octopus salad into my mouth. I don't know if it was the tentacles or the texture, but I had to excuse myself.

Stefania came after me. I wished she hadn't. She found me hugging the porcelain pony and started ranting in Italian and blessing herself. It seemed it was nearly sacrilegious to throw up the Christmas feast. I felt terrible. I just had to tell her about the baby. It was my only way out. While I washed up, I fessed up.

"Stefania, you can't tell a living soul. You're the only person I trust."

She leaned against the sink, starring at me with her perfect eyebrows vexed. Stefania could never have been a poker player. Her face always gave her thoughts away.

I wiped my mouth with a towel and whispered, "I'm pregnant."

She screamed with joy and wrapped me in a bear hug. You'd have thought it was the best news she'd ever heard. Then I told her who the father was. She went back to muttering in Italian and crossing herself.

Finally, she waved her hands in the air, as if she was shooing a pesky fly. "Forget him. It's still a celebration!" Tugging my arm, she dragged me back out to the dining room. Immediately after I'd sworn her to secrecy, she made a big announcement about my pregnancy in Italian so that everyone would get it the first time. The room erupted in cheers of *"Salute!"*

I avoided making eye contact with Francesco or any of the other men. It might have been my imagination, but for the rest of the night, they seemed less attentive after the news. At least I didn't have to worry about doing anything else I shouldn't do, especially on New Year's Eve. I swore Stefania and all of her relatives to silence. It wasn't as if any of them knew anyone else in my life.

The excitement of the Fortini family was downright contagious. I knew then that I just had to keep the baby. Besides, if I ever had an abortion and Gram learned of it, she'd have disowned me. I had considered giving the baby up for adoption. So many people are desperate for a child and unable to have one. Except once Jessie started growing inside of me I'd never be able to go through with giving her away. Before that night, I hadn't ever let myself think about what life might be like if I had an actual family of my own.

It was a blessing, if you thought about it, a chance to create life when so many people were dying, like the folks at Safe Harbor. Life is a gift certificate with an invisible expiration date. Every life comes with one but you just can't see it. My decision made, I had a new worry. What if like Dee, I was a horrible mother. I'd have to read like a fiend. I'd have to learn everything I could. Motherhood was not only miraculous it was terrifying.

CHAPTER NINE
Clairvoyance

And he said, Hear now my words: If there be a prophet among you, I the Lord will make myself known unto him in a vision, and will speak unto to him in a dream. —Numbers 12:6, KJV

Sleep is my only escape from this nightmare. Sometimes I have my favorite dream about Francesco. We're riding in the backseat of a mini convertible through Italy. The sun is lighting up the day and warm wind lifts my hair into the air while we wind down narrow roads on a hillside near water. At other times, I have nightmares that something evil is chasing me or trying to strangle me and I wake up gasping, screaming. I forget where I am.

English says he'll a put the gag back on me if I don't stop crying out. How can I? It's not something I control. English is feeding me more regularly now, but it seems like it has been a long time since he was here. I can't sense time passing anymore.

I wake up to music again, live music. They're playing some drums and a guitar. It starts and stops, loud at first before it falls silent. I drift off to sleep, but not for long before the drums wake me up again.

Spicy scent first, English comes in. He's calmer than he was during our last chat. Maybe he'll be the nice version of himself instead of his evil twin. He lifts my hands to put something in them.

"Here, I brought you some water."

"Thank you," I say, gulping it down. I'm so dry my eyes can't stop blinking.

I need a shower so badly. I'm nearly polluted. English unties my hands because there is no woman here to help me. Once the ties are off, he holds my hands and turns them over in his, rubbing my wrists. The music is back on. It's not Beethoven but something similar.

"You need medicine on these. After you bathe, I will do this. Provided you behave, I will leave them off. Keep the blindfold on until I close the bathroom door. I left you some towels, soap, and new clothes. Call out if you need anything else. When you finish, put on the clothes I left for you and bring the old clothes to me. Don't forget to replace the blindfold."

I shut the door, whip off the blindfold, and turn on the shower. With my hands free again, I think about smashing the window and running for it. My plan must be better than that. First, I need to get clean. I want to wash the smell of this place off me. My hair feels like straw. I let the warm water run over my face, tasting the soap that I've scrubbed all over myself; it's sweetly toxic. It reminds me, in Gram's generation they used to threaten to wash your mouth out with soap. For a moment, I wonder if you could you die from swallowing too much of it.

I'd like to stay in here but I don't dare take longer. When I'm done, I put on the clothes that he left for me. They are a sort of linen pajamas and not much different from the scrubs I've been wearing for days. How many days has it been now? I don't care what the clothes look like, as long as they're clean. I knock. English leads me back to my room. My wet hair hangs down, soaking the back of my new shirt, causing a chill through my body.

"Let's talk, Janice. Tell me what you know and how you know it."

"I'm sorry," I say. "What I told you is the truth. Please." I want to beg for my life and for Jessie's life. I want to know she's alright. "I didn't know exactly what was going to happen. I only knew people were going to get hurt or killed."

"It seems impossible to me that you have so little concern for your baby. I find it insulting that you would mock me after I have shown you such kindness. Since you refuse to be compliant, Janice, you force me to punish you."

He puts the wrist ties back on, even tighter this time. He calls out to one of the others. I don't have time to answer him before the door opens. By his odor, I know it's someone new who enters my closet jail. He reeks worse than patients who come to Safe Harbor after bad home care. I press my lips together tightly, but the smell becomes a nasty taste in my mouth.

They have a discussion in their language. I recognize some words here and there now, but not enough to understand what they're saying. Over time, I could get it, if I have more time that is.

There's a new sound. *Shree. Shree. Shree.* I know this sound. I've heard it before in the O'Neil's kitchen, when Stefania sharpened the kitchen knives. This is very kind of them. At least my death will be quick.

S*hree. Shree. Shree.*

This new guy has never even heard of deodorant. I'll call him Bo, short for B.O. or body odor. The smell is more intense now and the stench makes my eyes water. The sound is right in front of me. Bo is next to my bed. I suck in my breath. If these men are friends, you'd think one of them would say, "Hey, bro. You could really use a shower and some D.O. for your B.O."

Bo presses something cold against my neck. He's even less patient than English. He's here because English has failed. English translates and I hear it all twice. Focusing on the words, I wrap my brain around something other than death. He says the words, "can-thed," then "nah-be," and yells something at me that I can't understand. He bends the cold thing. I feel the blade on my neck. I know enough about anatomy to know where my jugular vein is. So does Bo.

English says something to him and then to me.

"I have convinced my brother to let you live for long enough to prove your claims. Unfortunately, he still wants to cut off your head or to at least remove your tongue."

I swallow hard. English continues.

"This is a predicament for me. I would like to let you live Janice. I might even believe you. If some sorcery allows you to know the path to the unknown, you will use this curse to do as we ask."

I suddenly remember how bad I am at tests. I hope to God that I'll pass this one. Bo pushes the knife harder against my neck. A trickle of blood slides down and I feel it pooling at my collarbone. I have to fight not to lose my lunch. My eyes start to water, but I refuse to cry. I won't show weakness. Fuck them.

English says something to Bo in a low voice. Bo moves back, letting up on the pressure of the knife but I can still feel it.

"Are you with the Jinn? Or are you a sorceress or a devil?"

I try to sound sure of myself, but my voice gives me away. "I don't know what that first thing is but my gift isn't evil. I'm a Catholic. The messages come from spirits or angels."

"What do these spirit angels tell you?"

"Important things," I say. "Sometimes they tell me about the past. Usually, it's about the future. I might know if someone's death is coming soon or if a person is in danger."

They discuss this and I hear certain words repeated, "Hassan" and "Ahmed." English asks me, "Do they say that my brothers and I will die? Do they say that you will die?"

I consider a lie then go with a form of truth instead.

"We'll all die someday," I say. "But I can't see my own death or even most important things that will happen to me. Like, I didn't know you were going take me."

"Why not?" he asks.

"The messages are about the fate of other people. In the visions, I see their faces. I can't know about your fate, whether I've seen your death coming, without seeing your faces."

"Many people make claims such as this," English says. "Most of them are liars. You look like a liar to me." I hear the squeal of the chair legs on the floor.

Bo slides the point of the knife up and down my throat, brushing my neck as if he's using a feather to tickle me. He leans in and whispers in my ear, "So-fa toola cab-be vota, mahl-moota."

English clears his throat, but he doesn't translate. He says something quietly to Bo. The door opens, then closes, and Bo's stench fades a little, but lingers.

"Pain has a way of making people see the truth more clearly, Za-hera. Don't you agree? I often find mental anguish is the best motivator." He strokes my face with his hand and then drops something onto the bed.

"I have a gift for you—something to inspire honesty and loyalty. I'll leave the light on for a little while."

And I'm alone again. Za-hera? Now I have a nickname. What's wrong with me? I had all of those days, when it was just English with me. I could have used the fork. I could be free right now. Then what would I do? I'd have to get away. I'd have to get back to Jessie. How far would I get?

Can I even kill someone or do any harm with a fork? Would I have the strength to finish the job if I started it? I don't know. I don't know anything anymore. I only know the secrets the spirits share with me.

Without sight, I only have the visions that don't come as often as I'd like them to. I only have shreds of my tattered faith. If they believe me, they might take off the blindfold and my chances of escape will improve.

English is right. I am a liar.

❖

On Christmas Day at the cottage, I told Gram all about my dinner with the Fortini family. She listened to me and never said a single word.

"If they invite me back next year, you should come with me."

"It would be my pleasure," she said. "I'll go if I'm available."

It was an odd thing for Gram to say. She only left the house to go to church, to the rectory or to the market. It wasn't as though her social calendar was full; so typical of Gram.

When we exchanged our gifts, I could tell she liked the statue. She held it up, looked at it for a long time, and then set it on the table. As the Catholic symbol of motherhood, the statue of Mary seemed appropriate. Gram was the only mother I'd ever known.

I opened the gift she had given me; a sweater she'd knit herself out of coffee-brown mohair with silver buttons running up the front. The color reminded me of Francesco's eyes and was warmly cozy when I slipped it on. The cottage was always freezing in the winter. Never meant to be a year-round home, it had no insulation.

We spent the rest of the day relaxing, playing cards, eating cinnamon toast, and sipping tea. We made puzzles and watched black-and-white movies. Later on, we stuffed and baked a small chicken for dinner and ate at four o'clock in the afternoon. By five-thirty, I went off to work the night shift. Gram went into the chapel.

❖

At Safe Harbor, I had the night from hell. Mr. Jameson filled diaper after diaper with diarrhea. It was like the worst package that kept on giving. The other CNA on duty got into Mel's stash and got stinking drunk. An hour into her shift, she passed out in one of the vacant patient rooms. As hard as I tried, I couldn't wake her up. Even after I threw an entire cup of water on her, she didn't budge. I was so furious that I left a note for Mel. I was running around like a maniac while I tried to stay on top of everything.

Mrs. Phillips fell down as she tried to make it to the restroom on her own without her walker. Thank the Lord, she didn't break a hip or do any real damage to herself. Still, I had to call the on-call doctor. He was furious and blamed me for her accident. On top of it all, I lost my Saint Agatha medal. It was hanging on a chain around my neck at the beginning of my shift. By the end of the night, it had disappeared. I only hoped it hadn't wound up in anyone's food.

Things finally settled down after midnight. The overnight shift ended at 6:00 a.m. on Sunday morning. The second I saw the day shift CNA, I bolted.

As soon as I stepped inside my apartment, I knew Rags had been alone for too long. I cleaned the cat box every week. I wasn't a careless pet owner, but his food dish was empty and he had left me two Christmas presents. One was on the bathroom rug, and the other was in the center of my bed.

I filled his food bowl, threw out the rug, cleaned up the cat scat on the bed, flipped the mattress, and changed the sheets. It was just what I felt like doing after changing beds and cleaning up crap all night. I seriously considered chucking Rags out into the hall, but then I reconsidered. It wasn't his fault. If I had even a drop of energy left, I might have felt sorry for myself. Instead, I crashed and didn't open my eyes again until noon.

❖

English said he left me a gift.

His ice water tone sends a quake through me. I edge up the blindfold. My eyes struggle to adjust to the bright, bare bulb hanging off the wire in the middle of the ceiling. I haven't seen the room totally lit before, but it's no more exciting than it is in the dark. Except now, I can read that the empty boxes in the corner came from an instrument store called Zounds. I stare down at the envelope on the bed next to me. The flap is open. I lift the corner and pictures slide out. I'm too petrified to see them just yet. I squeeze my eyes closed.

Open your eyes, Janice!

I can't open them. I'm afraid to see. Please don't make me look.

If you don't save them, who will?

I focus for just a few seconds and pull out the stack of pictures before tears flood my eyes and I become blind again.

❖

Another word for psychic ability and second sight is clairvoyance. At work, I sometimes had the overwhelming sense that a particular patient was doomed. Then next time I went in for my shift, that patient would be at the hospital. Any patient who traveled from Safe Harbor to the hospital was usually a goner.

It was too heavy a burden to carry alone. I needed to talk to someone about it. Despite her issues, Cilla's still a good listener. None of us is perfect. Some folks appear to have fewer problems or just get better genes or families. The gene pool is all a big crapshoot, but I like to think God tries to be fair about it. I'm naturally petite like Dee. I'm five feet two inches tall and slim. Looks were never my problem but the kids teased me for not having a mother, and about my old religious grandmother.

Nobody gets a free pass in this life. Most people take having parents for granted. I have my dad's exotic, almond-shaped, hazel eyes. His name was Miguel. I never met him but I know he worked on the docks in Baltimore, that he was supposedly wild about Dee and that she thought she was too good for him. One day, a shipping container crushed him flat. It was a freak accident. Dee made it all about her and got into a huge fight with his grieving relatives at the funeral. Dee was a real class act or so I've heard. The fight was about me and I wasn't even born yet.

Cilla has a perfectly normal family with two sisters and two parents who worry about her and call her constantly. I envy Cilla's family and her big brain. She goes to school in the mornings at the College of Southern Maryland to study nursing. After spending a fortune on her biology degree, which led her nowhere, Cilla's parents said the rest of her education would be on her dime. She'll be great, though. She's an excellent caregiver, and she already knows nursing. Even though Cilla is not officially qualified, Nurse Miller lets her do her work sometimes. On slow days, I would quiz Cilla about illness and anatomy.

"What's the superior vena cava?" I asked while we fixed meal trays for our patients. The factory odor of the food made me sick to my stomach. I wondered how the elderly choked it down. With old age, I imagine, you completely lose your sense of smell and your taste buds, along with everything else.

"It's the large vein that returns blood from the heart to the head, neck, and upper limbs," she answered easily. "All right, give me a tough one."

"Cilla, do you ever get the sense something is going to happen before it does?"

"Like what?"

"Like," I said. "Someone might die soon."

"Do you mean instinctually or by means of medical signs?"

"I mean like a vision or a psychic experience."

Cilla was too scientific to take my question at face value. She frowned as she considered it.

"Janice, I don't believe there is any scientific evidence to support psychic experiences. Having spent years working with people who are clearly at the ends of their lives, I do believe that people can develop excellent instincts for knowing when someone is near death." She went on.

"There are physical signs, after all, like reduced appetite and changes in blood pressure, pulse, breathing, and speech. Patients develop mottled skin and sometimes they may even experience hallucinations. Since you're such a sensitive person, you may be dwelling on death to such a degree that your subconscious mind makes it *seem* as though the information is coming from an outside source. You're really only reacting to the physical signs."

"I'm sure you're right," I said. "That must be it."

When it came to seeing the future, the biggest letdown of all was not seeing the things that mattered most. Why would they tell me about the imminent demise of someone I barely knew and then have been all tight-lipped about the people who were closest to me? I imagined the messengers thought I couldn't handle knowing, but it made me angry all the same.

Cilla's explanation seemed so logical that I accepted it for a while. Then one day, it happened again and in broad daylight. The voices were getting bolder. On my way to the O'Neil house, I was running late. My watch had stopped working again after I'd just put new batteries in it. Driving at a good clip, I skidded a few times. The ice in the early morning made the roads mirror slick. My rattling little car had seriously bald tires. I'd been meaning to replace them once I had the time and the money—in other words, never. Nearing the house, I heard a voice as clear as a bell. I looked around certain there was someone in the car with me, but nobody was there.

"Slow down, Janice," the voice said.

I was startled to such a degree I did what the voice said. Just then, a small child bundled up in winter clothes ran into the road and stood right in front of my car. I hit the brakes and slid to a stop inches away from her baby-doll face. Seconds later, her frightened mother was there scooping her up. The woman stared at me. She smiled a little and I saw the sense of relief spread over her face. If I hadn't heard the voice, I'd have still been speeding. I'd have surely hit that child and changed both our lives forever. So where on earth, did that voice come from? It came from nowhere on earth.

CHAPTER TEN
Consciousness

Cleaning out my car, I came across Annie Kellogg's business card. Maybe it was a sign. Lately, wasn't everything? I called her, figuring she was my last stop on the high-speed train to the hospital's loony wing.

Annie asked me over to her house on a gray Saturday in January. I was expecting some gypsy hut, but she lived in a big three-story modern house on the waterfront in Deale.

The fortuneteller business must be booming.

I sat in her driveway with my keys still in the ignition, debating whether to go in or not and watching the chop on the bay. A pair of ospreys circled and dove. One of them flew away with something dangling from its talons. Ospreys are excellent parents.

What the hell, I'll go in. What did I have to lose besides what was left of my damn mind. I was already convinced I was gonzo. With my arms crossed, I walked toward the front door. It was a pretty shade of blue with etched glass. Annie opened it before I could knock. She wore a genuine smile on her slim face.

"Janice, I'm so glad you could make it. Please, come in."

Her home was airy and inviting with seaside décor: tall wooden cranes and jars filled with beach glass. In the entryway, a large painting of a blue heron hung on the wall. A local artist painted it. I recognized the name. Annie had good taste.

I'd made a list of questions on a piece of paper, which I'd tucked into my jacket pocket. I patted it to make sure that it was still there.

"I expected you'd call sooner, but you must not have been ready. How are you feeling?"

"Fine," I said. It would have been true if "fine" and "freaked out" were synonymous. I had called and hung up three times before letting the phone ring long enough for her to pick it up.

"You've been on my mind ever since our meeting in the store," she said as she led me into a sunken living room.

An assortment of religious statues was perched on her mantel. They had definitely come from the store where we met. Among others, Saint Anthony and Saint Catherine were there, looking down on us mortals. Annie watched me as I took it all in.

"Can I get you something?" She asked. "Coffee? Water? A snack?"

"Sure," I said. "I'd like a glass of water, please."

Out of curiosity, I was tempted to take her up on her offer of a snack, wondering if they were fancy snacks like the ones Claire served.

"You have a lovely home," I said.

"Thank you. Please, Janice, make yourself comfortable," she said, gesturing toward a beefy cream-colored couch and an L-shaped love seat. I was too jittery to sit down. When she went into the kitchen, I did some more snooping around. Behind the couch, the back wall of the living room was made of paneled glass. Sliders led to a large deck.

The rain clouds that had been threatening us all day started to spit at the windows. On the deck, drops bounced and rolled off the covered furniture. Two Adirondack chairs sat empty on the lawn, which rolled straight down to a rock wall with the bay on the other side. I looked, but I didn't see any sign of the ospreys.

"I assume you would like a reading," Annie said, carrying two crystal glasses over to the coffee table. She set the glasses down and sat on the loveseat with her legs tucked under her.

"Sure," I said. "I guess." I walked over, perched on the edge of the couch and waited. At the center of the table sat a wooden box, carved by hand and etched with birds and butterflies. She opened the box and took out a deck of playing cards with pictures of ornate women on them. I wasn't interested in getting involved with the occult. If she was that kind of psychic, I was going to leave.

"I don't like witchcraft or anything, though," I said.

"Janice, I can assure you, neither do I. My work is all about spirituality, spirit guides, angels, and beings of light. These are angel cards, not tarot cards. The messages are positive. While there are warnings to help you protect yourself from potential harm, there are no curses or evil cards. If you're comfortable, we can use the cards. If not, I'll try to offer my guidance without them." She waited for my answer.

"I guess it's OK, as long as it's safe," I said.

Annie picked up the deck of angel cards and held them in her hands. She closed her eyes for a moment. I guessed that she was praying. Then she laid the deck of cards on the table between us. She asked me to shuffle and handle the deck until I felt comfortable. When I was ready, I placed them back on the table.

"Now, cut the deck four times, making a row of four small piles," she said.

When I was done, each stack displayed a different beautiful angel. Beginning with the stack closest to me, Annie turned over the top card on each pile, one at a time.

"Hmm," she said. "Do you want to know everything? Even the warning signs?"

"For now, let's just stick with whatever is the most positive." I hoped my luck would turn around soon, but it never seemed to. I was careful not to say anything that was overly expressive. Phonies can take your signals and use the information against you.

I took a long drink of the water. Fancy glasses even made water taste better. Annie looked at the cards and then at me. I didn't care for the look on her face. She wouldn't have been any better at poker than Stefania.

"OK," Annie said. "Maybe we should we start with the questions that you came here to ask."

I looked at my pocket. The note wasn't sticking out. "You mean there's no good news?"

"There is good news, but I'm afraid that it's tied to concerning news."

"OK," I said. "Spill it."

"Are you sure?"

"I came here, didn't I?"

She sighed. "You'll have an opportunity to aid a large number of people. In the process, though, your personal safety will be at risk. The outcome is unclear. I've been instructed to give you a message."

"What's the message?" I asked.

"Stop fighting it and learn to accept the role that you've been given."

"What does that mean?"

"I don't know," she said. "They say that you know."

"But I don't know," I got up and paced around the room. "Who are they? What do they want? And why me?" The rain poured down pinging off the windows. Lightening lit up the bay. I'd come to Annie for answers, not more questions.

"This comes from your spirit guides. I'm afraid I don't know exactly what they are trying to tell you. Sometimes you have to piece several messages together like a puzzle in order to get the full picture."

"But the problem is, I don't speak spirit," I said exasperated.

"Try not to get upset. It's not good for the baby. I'll help you in any way that I can, Janice. You aren't alone in this."

I was having trouble breathing. I sat down and stared at the cards. Annie was quiet for a moment. Then she asked, "What are your questions? Maybe we can try to get there through another method."

"Well," I said. "When something is bothering me, I sometimes feel like I get answers from someplace other than my own mind. Is that how spirit guides talk?"

She nodded.

"When I start to think that it's crazy," I continued, "I'll see something, but not a ghost or anything, more like a sign. Only, it's not in my imagination, it's in real life, like a road sign or a post that looks like a cross or a statue. It makes me feel like I'm not crazy, like this is real."

"Yes," she said. "It's good. Your awareness and consciousness will continue to grow that way."

My consciousness? I wasn't interested in becoming more aware. I wanted to fix this thing. I wanted to do whatever I had to do to make it stop.

"Oh," I said. "And I've started having trouble with my jewelry."

"How so?" She asked.

"Things are breaking," I said. "I'm losing things. My watches stop working all the time."

"Jewelry and personal items hold onto energy. Try putting some quartz in your jewelry box, and avoid wearing secondhand jewelry before clearing the original owner's energy."

"How do I do that?"

"I'll make some notes for you."

She suggested I research the other gemstones, but she said Lapis Lazuli would help me see things more clearly.

"With the watch stopping," she said, "time may be significant. Whenever this happens try to tune into everything going on around you."

"I already lost my Saint Agatha medal," I said. "It kept coming off its chain. Once I found it in my bed and the clasp that held it together wasn't even open. Another time, I was walking through the parking lot at work, and the chain just flew off my neck and hit the ground. The last time it just vanished."

Her expression changed. A slight frown formed on her pale lips. "I need to teach you some clearing exercises and protection prayers."

"What're those?" I asked.

"A clearing is a type of prayer that you can use to get rid of negative energy."

I was still unsure the whole thing wasn't just a bunch of hocus-pocus. Before my jewelry trouble, I might have put it all out of my mind. I wondered if people with similar experiences ignored them or thought their minds were playing tricks on them.

"Janice, I'd like you to keep a journal of anything that seems unusual. When you go back and review it, you'll see patterns develop. This will help decode the messages. It may take time to understand them clearly, but they usually send them in a familiar way. For example, I love sailing. My references usually have to do with boating and the sea. You can also ask questions. Quite often you'll get answers back."

I was glad I came but more worried than before talking to Annie. She never asked me for money and when I offered, she refused to take it.

"It's obvious to me," she said. "We were destined to meet. Our channels have crossed for a reason."

By nature, I'm suspicious, but I decided she seemed on the level, albeit a level where most people never ventured. She made some decaffeinated coffee. We sat and talked for a little longer and waited for the storm to pass.

"Why do you do it?" I asked. "How did you know you should?"

"I always felt there was something different about me even when I was a child. I sensed certain things about people and their emotions would sometimes manifest in me. In the beginning, it was especially difficult to be around children because they're so emotive. If they would cry, so would I. Then I learned how to manage it."

"How?" I asked.

"It's a process. You have to forge your own path and grow at your own spiritual pace. You can train yourself not be so open all of the time. Reading is a good way to enhance your understanding. Ask for guidance when you look for books."

"You mean ask for guidance from the librarian?"

She shook her head no and pointed at the ceiling.

"Ah," I said. "Gotcha."

She touched my arm adding, "I don't want to scare you, but communicating with spirits is not always positive. You need to be careful."

What? Now I had to watch out for evil in the spirit world as well as on earth. This was just great. I had a new problem.

"Isn't this, like a sin?" I asked.

"No, Janice. You may be surprised how much assistance you could receive from the church on this. Prophecy is nothing new to religion. If you feel comfortable, I recommend you go see a priest for further insight."

I just happened to know a few priests.

Annie's parting advice was clear. "Don't fear it. At the same time, though, you should try not to own it. Strive to focus less on the destination and more on the journey and you'll feel more at peace with it."

I thanked her and she said I should come to see her anytime. I considered that maybe I was reading too much into my experiences. If Annie had it and I had it, then other people would also have it. It was just another trait from the gene pool. Like freckles, it was no big hairy deal.

As I drove home, I sang along to "She Talks to Angels." It was funny that this song was on the radio just then.

❖

I say a prayer before looking at the pictures in the envelope. When I finally look, I can't catch my breath. I feel like I'm on a roller coaster moving too fast. I want to get off this ride, but the controller is a carnie who's missing too many teeth and enjoying scaring the crap out of me.

At first, I think my eyes aren't adjusting. Then, I see that the photos are black and white. The first is a picture of Bridge and Jessie. They're in the hall of the rectory. The image is blurry, but I know it's my baby. She's beautifully fragile and wrapped her receiving blanket. Her little head pokes out, covered in baby fuzz. Bridge is in her habit, smiling and cradling Jessie. I hug the picture to my chest before laying it on the bed.

The second photo is of Cilla wearing scrubs. She's walking to her car in the parking lot at Safe Harbor. Next, there's a shot of Stefania smoking on the back steps behind the kitchen of the O'Neil home. Then, there's a picture of Annie with a man on a sailboat. There's another picture of Mrs. S. pushing a shopping cart around the local market.

The last photo, taken at a strange angle, I can't make out at first. It looks like an aerial view of road-kill, something gray and white with something darker pooling out around the dead animal. Then I recognize the background as the sidewalk in front of my apartment. The lifeless pile of fur is Rags.

Behind the photo, I feel a note card. It has just one line scrawled on it:

We will start with the oldest and work our way back.

The door cracks open. A hand slips in and switches out the light. Through the door English says, "It's bedtime now, Janice, pleasant dreams."

As if I could sleep. The bastard! Bile burns the back of my throat. I never thought I could possibly hate anyone more than Jason or entertain murderous thoughts about a stranger.

English and his pals are terrorists. They're like the terrorists that everyone hears about on the news. My instincts were completely wrong, to not initially sense a dangerous vibe coming from English.

I can thank my judgment when it comes to men. It's always been somewhat skewed. Where are you, my guides?

He has my keys. He's been in my apartment. He's followed my friends. He killed my cat.

I hope Rags didn't suffer too much. If English had thrown him from the second floor, Rags could have lived. English must have killed him first and then tossed him out the window. I only hope Mrs. S. didn't see Rags that way. Oh no. *We'll start with the oldest.* I have to stop them.

They were planning some heinous attack on the tunnel, and I messed things up for them without even knowing it. I'm glad I wrecked their plans. Now I just have to get them before they get my friends.

I hear a car door slam shut and an engine rev up. Tires skid on gravel. Someone just left in a hurry. So how many are still here with me. I walk to the wall and press my ear against it. There's no music. The television is on. Maybe they always leave it on to trick me into thinking I'm not alone. It sounds like the news.

When he was in my apartment, did he leave any clues? Did anyone see him? There is always hope.

I'm in terrible need of a shower again and I want to hold my baby. I'm not usually a crier, but I can't stop this squall of tears from coming down. I wish I had Cilla's brains so I could figure a way out of this mess. I wish I had Stefania's confidence or Annie's insights.

I press my ear up against the wall again and listen to the muffled news report.

"Cold. Cold. Cold. That's tonight's forecast, Jay, and there is no end in sight. It's unseasonable even for November. Over to you."

It's still November. It hasn't been that long then, has it?

"Thanks, Marcia. Now for our top story tonight. There is still no word on the missing North Beach woman, Janice Morrison. Townspeople have gathered this evening for a vigil at Saint Mary's

Church led by the Sisters of Mercy. The search continues tomorrow morning."

Ape mutters something. I hear the news reporter say, "You're watching ABC News in Baltimore." Before Ape changes the channel and I hear, "That's right, John. Our three final contestants are ready to enter the wipeout zone…"

Goosebumps spread like a virus over my body. Shivering, I slump to the floor. I'll fight for my life and for my friends. They are looking for me. I just have to have faith.

CHAPTER ELEVEN
Ironic

Thou shalt not bear false witness against thy neighbour. —Exodus 20:16, KJV

By mid February, at eight weeks pregnant, the scale was still my friend. Jessie developed slowly and secretly. According to the baby development pictures I found on the internet, Jessie still didn't weigh much more than a guppy and looked more alien than human. She'd be growing little earlobes soon. I'd really have to watch my mouth.

I'd found a doctor a little late. I went to my first of a dozen appointments. Doctor Williams and I eventually came to an understanding, but I could tell from the start he'd be challenging. He struck me as judgmental. I later discovered he liked having the last word. I'm sure you know the type.

He peered down at me over his wire-rimmed glasses with his gray hair sticking out in all directions and asked, "Will the baby's father be present for any of the appointments?"

"No, he will not," I answered in a matter-of-fact tone. There was no need to get into things that were none of his business. He raised one bushy eyebrow, but dropped the subject. I imagine he thought I was just another ignoramus who had gotten pregnant on purpose. This couldn't have been further from the truth. I had planned to be an informed mother-to-be. I had started reading voraciously, everything I could find about pregnancy and childbirth. That's how I am when I get my mind set on something.

Gram always said, "There's no excuse for ignorance, as long as there are books to be read."

As the weeks went by, it wasn't easy to keep quiet. I couldn't risk talking to Stefania about the baby for fear that Claire might overhear. I hadn't spilled the beans to Cilla yet.

I did tell Cilla about all of my strange new insights and about my meeting with Annie. Cilla still wanted to argue on the side of science, but she took my case on as a study in psychology, for one of her classes.

"So, Janice, tell me some more examples of your spooky experiences," she said one day. "I have to say that I find your malady fascinating."

We were changing Mrs. Carlson's sheets while Mrs. C. was playing bingo in the common room. I gave Cilla an earful.

"I was watching TV a few weeks ago," I said, "and the newscaster with the bad comb-over came on." She nodded. "He was talking about the economy and blah, blah, blah. Suddenly, I froze. I stared at the screen while these thoughts shot through my brain like lightning bolts. I knew then that he was going to die. I felt there was something about his upper body in the chest area. That was it."

"So," she said. "What happened?"

"A few nights later, I turned on the same channel. The anchorwoman was there, but the man wasn't. The woman said, 'Our thoughts and prayers are with the family of our co-worker.'"

"What happened?" Cilla asked.

"He had died of a heart attack," I said.

Cilla's face turned as white as the sheet we were putting on the bed. I'm not sure she had really believed me before then. Cilla clutched a pillow and took a seat on the bed. "Janice, what does this mean? That's just freaky."

"I know," I said. "I felt sick to my stomach. There are so many occurrences now I can't keep track of them all. I write them down now. See for yourself."

I handed her my journal. I usually kept it tucked into the waistband of my scrubs. After reading a few entries, Cilla looked up at me, horrified.

"I think that we should keep this to ourselves," she said with her face so pale even her freckles were lighter. "You may need to talk to a real psychiatrist or maybe even a priest. Surrounded by such sorrow every day, you might be severely depressed. Don't take this the wrong way, but could you be inventing some of this?"

"Look at the journal, Cilla," I said. "What do you think?"

As she read a few more pages, a grave expression spread over her face.

"Gosh. You're scaring me, Janice."

"Holy shit, Cilla, I'm scaring myself!"

For a smart girl, Cilla could be annoyingly naïve. I needed to talk to someone about all of this, but I didn't want that someone to be a shrink and get myself locked up while knocked up. At best, I had a borderline faith in doctors. I wasn't keen on having them poking at my body or my mind. What would I do if I were crazy? I'd end up in a home somewhere. Even if I deserved it, those places are worse than nursing homes.

If you're truly crazy, you supposedly think you're sane. If you think you're crazy, on the other hand, you're actually not. Now, wouldn't this make us all one big can of mixed nuts?

I had told Bridge about some of my experiences. She didn't seem to think I was crazy. I decided I could go straight to the top and talk with the priest. They had to keep whatever you told them under their collars. Ever since I was in elementary school, Gram and I were regulars at St. Mary's, where Gram worked. I knew the priest, Father Ballentine, very well.

On Saturdays, Gram and some of the other parish women volunteered to clean the church. I helped until I was old enough to stay at home on my own. I always loved the church's old wood smell mixed with Murphy's oil soap and incense.

Throughout the years, the parish fathers were like kind uncles to me so I never felt strange about asking them questions. Our current priest, Father B., was my favorite. Still, I wondered if I might be a tiny bit nervous about talking to him about this particular phenomenon. What if Annie was wrong and the premonitions were the work of the devil? I called the rectory and got in touch with Bridge.

"What's new, Janice? I haven't seen you in a long time."

"I know. I miss our chats." In truth, I'd been avoiding her. Bridge had a way of seeing right through me. I didn't want to tell her about Jessie until I'd had a chance to tell Gram; something else I was avoiding.

"Well don't be such a stranger. Did you need to talk to Beatrice?"

Beatrice Morrison. What a relief Dee didn't name me after Gram.

"No," I said. "Actually, if you could keep this between us, I need to see the big man."

"Of course," she said.

I was long overdue for a confession. If I chickened out on sharing my newfound prophecy, there was always time for reconciliation.

"Let's see," she said. "Oh, he's booked for the next week or so. Then he has the parish trip to Italy the second week in March. If it's urgent, I could squeeze you in before he goes away."

"No," I said. "That's all right. It can wait." I was lying, of course.

"OK," she said. "I've got you down for the first Saturday in April."

"Thanks, Bridge. I'll talk to you soon." At that point, my pregnancy would be fourth months along. Would I be showing? I certainly didn't want to discuss my pregnancy with Father B. before I told Gram.

❖

Cilla suggested I read up on premonitions and forecasting the future. She recommended some experts on this sort of thing. She mentioned Carl Jung who I was surprised to discover wasn't Chinese. She also mentioned Edgar Cayce, known as the sleeping psychic because he went into a trance state whenever he received messages from the great beyond.

I'm not exactly a library person. I always felt like an impostor when I was in a library. I worried I might break some major library rule that everyone knew but me. I envisioned the library officials would point to the door and ask me to leave the premises and never return.

On Saturday, I took a quick trip to the library in town. The first thing I did was lie to the librarian. "I'm working on a paper for school. It's about psychics and psychic phenomenon."

"Oh," the librarian said leading me. "Well, we have a small section over here. If there's anything else that I can help you with, just let me know."

Oddly, the religious books were in the same section. I picked up a few of them, including a book about world religions. I didn't know much about any religions, other than Catholicism. On my way to the desk, I grabbed a few books on pregnancy and childbirth.

"My friend is having a baby." The lies were just sliding off my tongue like hot butter. "I said I'd get her some books while I was picking up my research materials for school."

"Oh, how nice," she said, smiling. What a heel I was. I kept on lying to the librarian, when she seemed so nice. She didn't know me from Eve. She'd have no way to know I was being untruthful. That's why liars are mean. The other person automatically trusts you, and meanwhile you're not trustworthy. I made a mental note on my brains 'right and wipe board' to make up for my deceit by doing something kind. I had to even out my sinful scoreboard. Around then, my score tilted heavily to the sinful side.

What could I do? I couldn't have the librarian thinking I read about this stuff for my own interest. Rumors spread like cockroaches in a small town. Can you imagine all of the personal things librarians all over the world learn about people based on their book choices? They have good memories too. They remember where all of the books belong.

They're not unlike pharmacists. One time, I had to get medicine for a completely disgusting female ailment. The pharmacist was a young dude. He handed me my prescription and then asked, "Do you have any questions?"

"No," I said. I was already mortified. I just wanted to get the heck out of there. Then he started describing in detail how to apply the medicine. I turned eighty shades of red. The creep looked like he was enjoying my misery. I grabbed the brown paper sack he handed me, and I tore out of there. I've avoided his pharmacy ever since then and have to drive twenty minutes south to the Rite Aid in Prince Frederick. I curse him every time I have to fill a prescription. Cilla said what he did was illegal and I should have reported him. I was just too embarrassed.

❖

As bad as that was, I'd rather live through that again than remain imprisoned here for another day. I wake up on the floor; aching all over. I'm wondering about the window in the bathroom and if it's big enough for me to fit through it. Maybe. I could always go on a hunger strike and slim down more.

Even if I get away though, how far can I get? They know about my life. I tap on the wall for English to take me to the facilities. When he comes in, he doesn't even mention the pictures. He just says he'll bring my breakfast when I'm finished in the bathroom. I sneak a peek out the bathroom window. It's black as bleak outside. Why am I eating breakfast at night? I put my ear up to the bathroom wall. The evening news is on again. The bastards are messing with me.

Back in my closet-jail, I keep this in mind.

"Tell me what you know about our new plan?" English asks.

"I don't know anything."

"You claim to know the future, yet you deny knowing something so vital to your survival?"

"It doesn't work that way," I say. "I have to be somewhere. I have to see something first."

"But you are here, where the plan is being made. You can't be any closer to it."

"I want to tell you," I say. "I wish I could tell you."

"As do I, Janice. You disappoint me."

Why should you be any different from everyone else in my life?

❖

After weeks of pouring over the huge stack of library books, I was beginning to get a sense of my multiple dilemmas. On the positive side, I was able to track Jessie's growth and development. Then again, in doing so I realized I was running out of time to hide. I focused on my spiritual issues.

On the one hand, I felt important pretending to be a student. I was learning. I guess you could say I was a student of God. My Internet searches had led to some fascinating discoveries. I'd never realized how similar religion and some of the topics discussed in the paranormal texts were.

According to the bible, a prophet is a man who speaks on God's behalf in a relatable manner because he's concerned about the problems of the world during his lifetime. He sometimes predicts the future. Was prophecy part of God's plan for me? Out of millions of other humans, had he picked me? The notion was outrageous. Could God be the one talking to me? Was I some sort of prophet? It just couldn't be. I was grossly unqualified.

According to one book, angels were the messengers of God. Were the angels calling to leave me messages? If so, what was I supposed to do with the information?

In the paranormal texts, I read about the mysterious, all-seeing third eye located in the middle of the forehead. According to many religions, this was where your heart, mind, and body could simultaneously open up to a higher consciousness. I touched the spot on my own forehead. I didn't feel anything.

As usual, I had more questions than answers and my head hurt from thinking about it all. I needed a break, so I started chatting online with an old high school friend, Ken Parker. Ken was the valedictorian of my class and was like a male version of Cilla. He lived in Virginia and worked for the CIA; they recruited him right out of George Washington University. I had no idea what he did for them. We never discussed it. I only knew he worked in some office and that he wasn't a super secret spy.

We'd been friends ever since he tutored me in algebra and I'd discovered that he was 'crushing' on me. Math left my brain more confused than it was to begin with. With his help, I worked up from having an F to having a C in the class but felt like a dope. Ken tried to cheer me up.

"Janice, you're pretty on the inside and on the outside. You don't know how rare that is," he said.

It was the kindest thing any boy had ever said to me. Sadly, I had no better taste in boys back then than I do now. I was dating a burnout named Rusty. Rusty spent more time outside of school than he spent inside. It was a darn shame I couldn't force myself to be attracted to Ken.

"Aren't you just a doll," I said. The nickname stuck since Barbie's husband went by the same name. At the time, Ken looked like a giant stick insect. His glasses made his eyes bug out, so the nickname was funny.

"Not really, Janice," he said. "But I like when you're ironic."

I had to look up what ironic meant. Inspired by Ken's smarts, this started me on my routine of looking up one new word per day. Later on, Ken got contact lenses and started working out until he actually became Barbie's perfect mate. It truly was ironic. Of course, the girl I fixed him up with was no Barbie doll. I started out our online chat with a tease:

"Sup, Ken doll?"

"Hey, Janice the Menace. Staying out of trouble?"

"Where's the fun in that?"

"THNX for the intro. Pricilla is sweet."

"Bhave w/my BF."

"U no me. I'm 2 nice."

"Don't go changing."

"Do I have a choice? What R U up 2?"

"Work. It SUX."

"4Me 2."

"Yeah, but U R not MTing bedpans."

"BYTM. But I do have bad days with bad guys."

"Any I'd like?"

"U R hopeless, Janice."

"Yep. Yawn. B4N. Kiss Barbie GNITE."

"I wish."

❖

With all of my research filed into my brain, I lay in bed feeling as worn out as my jeans. Despite the crazy tricks my mind was playing on me, I knew life could have been worse. I was young and fairly, healthy. I still had some blessings left to count. Through the blinds, I watched a streetlight make shadow angels in my messy room. Rags, my furry foot warmer, curled up at my feet with his head tucked into his tail. With my third eye firmly fixed on the future, I drifted off to sleep.

CHAPTER TWELVE
Involuntary

My scrubs were on the baggy side so hiding Jessie remained my master plan for as long as possible. Then the terrible morning sickness began, more like morning, noon and night sickness. Even so, I'd managed to avoid any episodes at work.

I was in Mr. Jameson's room one day, changing his bedding, while he sat in his chair reading. While I worked, I felt his rodent eyes critically dart up from his book, watching me. The temperature in the room had to be eighty degrees. Beads of sweat rolled down my forehead.

"Watch my things on the end table, Missy," he said. "If you break anything, it will come out of your pathetic salary."

The crotchety old fart. Then, just like that, I had to hurl. He was still grumbling at me when I sprinted into his bathroom. There was no hiding my activity. Even without his hearing aid, he heard me retching.

I cleaned and disinfected the bathroom. When I came out, he peered over his reading glasses and fixed his beady eyes on me. He said, "You're in trouble now, girlie. I'm telling Mel."

"I'm very sorry, Mr. Jameson. I must have caught a bug or something."

"Humph! I doubt that very much. Too much of the hooch is more like it. You'll be sorry later, that's all I know."

Of all patients, it had to happen in his room. I cursed that wrinkled old bone-bag. I know that was mean, but seriously, couldn't I ever catch a break? I had to sweat it out for the rest of the day. Ten minutes before the end of my shift, I still hadn't heard anything. I thought maybe the old coot had fallen senile, but I had no such luck. Mel caught me in the hallway.

"Janice," she said. "I need to see you for a minute."

"Sure thing, Mel." *Crap on a half shell.* I followed her into her office.

"So, tell me what happened today in Mr. Jameson's room?"

"I'm really sorry, Mel. I was out with some friends last night, and I had a few too many drinks. I swear it won't happen again." I figured she of all people would be forgiving of that.

"See that it doesn't happen again, Janice. I'll have to write you up."

I didn't say a word; I just thought of a few. That rotting, old fossil, I wished he could have kept his shriveled pie hole shut. I had a good mind to put some Visine in his tapioca.

Instead, I convinced Cilla to trade me one of her heinous patients for Mr. Jameson. She was glad to give me Mr. Bates, the resident pervert. We had nicknamed him Master Bates since he wasn't shy about showing off his manly parts. He especially enjoyed making Cilla squirm. When he flashed his privates to me, I just acted as if I saw that sort of thing every day. It seemed like a fair trade.

On the upside, Mel still didn't know jack about my problem. It didn't seem right, though, to hide Jessie from Cilla anymore. At dinner in the cafeteria, Cilla wanted to know what was happening with the 'spooky' thing going on inside my head. I filled her in on my freaky slide shows.

"When I close my eyes, all of these faces fly at me in the dark. I can barely sleep."

"Gosh," she said. "You mean like disembodied heads?"

"I hadn't really thought about that. They're definitely not decapitated heads. Maybe I just don't see the bodies because I'm too focused on their faces."

"Are you sure you don't know any of these people?"

"I don't think so. Maybe I see them when I'm going about my business and my brain makes mental photo albums without my permission. Who knows?"

"I'm worried about you, Janice. You really need to see someone about this."

"I know. I'm working on it."

Cilla ate a mouthful of salad. There was no sign of her usual dietary staples: cheeseburger, onion rings, and a milkshake.

"Look at you eating health food," I said.

"Yeah, I guess. I have some new inspiration."

Playing stupid, I said, "Oh, yeah. What's up?"

"Ken's taking me out on a date Saturday. He's coming all the way down to pick me up, and then we're going to Annapolis for lunch."

"Cilla, that's great! Ken is a super nice guy." I was truly happy for them both.

"I know. Why didn't you ever go out with him?" She asked, scowling at a piece of lettuce.

"I don't know. We've always just been friends. Speaking of friendship, I have to tell you something, Cilla. You have to swear you won't breathe a word to anyone—not even Ken."

"I swear," she said, using her finger to cross her heart like a kindergartener. Her eyes grew saucer-wider while she waited for me to spill the gossip. I put on my most serious face.

"No one," I said. "And I mean no one."

"I swear. May God strike me down," she said, pointing up to heaven and crossing her heart for a second time.

"If Mel finds out, I'm toast," I added.

"Janice, I said I swear!"

"I'm pregnant," I blurted out, Janice style.

"Oh, my God!" Cilla clasped her hands over her mouth.

"I know," I said through a mouthful of fries.

"How many weeks?"

"About ten."

"Janice! Why didn't you tell me?"

"I don't know," I said. *Liar. Liar. Ass on fire.*

"Who's the father?"

"That's the worst part," I said. "It's Jason."

"Oh boy." She picked at my food, so I swatted her hand away.

"Sorry," she said. "Stress makes me eat."

"Tell me about it. Listen, Mel cannot find out about this. I'll be fired and I need my job and my health insurance."

"Janice, Mel can't legally fire you for being pregnant."

"Maybe not," I said. "But it's the part about the baby's daddy that would get me fired."

Cilla wrinkled her nose. "Oh, yeah. That's true. What were you thinking?"

"Cilla, I'm not at all sure I was."

❖

I've been using the facilities every chance I get. I'll do anything to get out of the musty room and work on my escape plan. English finally gave me some toiletries but he inspects them regularly. I don't doubt he expects me to act like a prisoner and make a shiv out of my toothbrush. One thing about prisoners like me, we have tons of time to think in devious ways.

The bathroom window here is just like the ones in Gram's cottage. There are twelve individual miniature panes. Yesterday I looked out the gap in the black paper covering to see a row of trees standing between this house and the next. These towering guards still have a few leaves that are the color of flame. They'll be my timekeepers now.

Just like this one, the window in my bedroom at Gram's house was nailed shut from the outside, dating back to when it was Dee's room. When I was ten-years-old, I picked at the caulk around one of the panes until the glass fell out into my hand. Then, I gulped in deep breaths of fresh air before I popped the glass back in.

So Gram wouldn't see what I'd done, I stuck a piece of chewing gum there and reapplied a fresh piece whenever the gum got too old to hold. Winter drafts always reminded me of my dirty deed. Still, I liked knowing the only thing keeping me from the outside world was a little bit of bubble gum, easy enough to remove.

A year later, I swiped a pack of cigarettes from my friend's mom and smoked them all in my room, blowing the smoke out of the little open square in the window. By the time I was thirteen years old, I'd already quit smoking due to the expense and how it made my hair and clothes stink. I still miss it sometimes, holding fire in my hand and breathing smoke like a dragon.

❖

English checks my toiletries. Once I pass inspection, he leads me into the bathroom. I close the door and turn on the water. Then I run my hand over the caulk and hatch a plan. I sense they will not kill me today, but I can't sit and wait for it, now can I?

Silently, English takes me back to the room. I keep asking questions but he refuses to answer. Tonight, he brings me water but no food. Between hunger and worry, I'm weak. I might just get thin enough to slip out the window. Right now, all I can think about is sleep.

CHAPTER THIRTEEN
Cryptograms

Then spake Jesus again unto them, saying, I am the light of the world: he that followeth me shall not walk in darkness, but shall have the light of life. —John 8:12, KJV

I kept hoping Jason would stay at school forever. Maybe you could make things happen by wishing. The worry of seeing him again made me as jumpy as a cat in a dog kennel. Soon my body would give up one of my secrets, and Jason might rub two of his brain cells together. Or not. He wasn't necessarily bright enough to figure out the baby was his.

Anyway, I had other things to agonize about. I was making good on saving money and working so much I didn't have time to think about anything else. Then I started getting the forewarnings all of the time about total strangers—people I'd seen on television or people I'd met in stores.

It was like someone had flicked a switch in my brain. Suddenly, I knew all of these things I had no business knowing. Somebody else's thoughts were vibrating inside of my head. I had always thought it would be amazing to know the future, but it was mostly just frightening and annoying. Plus, it made me feel a little ashamed. Who was I to have all of this personal and private knowledge?

If visual sight is like a window which you see the world through, second sight is like a shade that comes down over your mind. Then a slide show or a movie plays there and no matter how hard you try to, you can't change the channel or close your eyes. Your third eye is always wide open.

Despite what Annie said, I continued to fight it and tried like crazy to convince myself it was all in my imagination. Only every time I thought that way, something else would happen that would prove what I was seeing and hearing was real. The notebook I'd been keeping to document my psychic experiences was nearly full.

One day in March, I was in the checkout line at the supermarket next to a man who was in his late eighties. *Good for him, he's out buying groceries on his own.* He caught me watching him. Just then, a voice in my head said, "He'll be with us soon."

Us who? I looked around but I didn't see anyone or hear anything else. *So much for the spirits answering my questions.* I felt chills that started at the back of my neck and traveled all the way down to my toes.

It sounds crazy to hear someone else's voice inside your head. When you're talking to yourself in your mind, the voice always sounds like you. You recognize the thoughts as your own. Believe me, I would not have made up these strange thought on my own.

If the voices had told me to harm someone, I would have checked myself in at the loony bin. They didn't. I was still standing in line and must have made a face. The man locked eyes with me, as if he knew what I knew. I wondered if people became more psychic as they got closer to death. Would this mean I was dying too?

The man had the most serene expression, mixed with surprise and a little fear. I'll forever have his face burned into my brain. With my eyes, I tried to tell him that everything was OK.

When it was my turn at the register, the sales clerk was having all sorts of difficulty with her scanner. Then the credit card machine started to go haywire.

"That's weird," she said. "I haven't had a problem all day."

She had her arm wrapped with an Ace bandage. Another message came to me like a flash of lightning: "Her boyfriend hurts her."

Makeup covered up the remains of faded bruises on her face. She couldn't get the card machine to work, and the line behind me snaked around the market. I started to hyperventilate. I pulled out all of my cash to pay for my small basket of groceries, and sprinted out of there. Maybe I should have done something to help her. That thought still haunts me.

Speaking of haunting, I'd read that spirits can wreak havoc on electronic devices. It has something to do with them being all made out of energy. Wonderful, so now Spirits were following me around the grocery store and whispering things in my ear. I only hoped I wouldn't start seeing them next.

I hated not having control over what was happening to my body and my mind. Father B. was still traveling around Italy. Maybe I should've gone with him. I could've stayed there; and been a runaway. Only how do you run away from your own mind? I checked the listings for psychiatrists in the area to see if any of them worked on a sliding scale.

❖

I wake up to the hum of an engine and the sound of the tires on the driveway stones again. A car door opens and slams, the front door creaks and heavy feet pound the floor. Outside of my room, Ape and English bark at each other. It's just how they communicate. I stand with my body against the wall, listening to their language. Tonight, I'm sure they're talking about me. I hear Ape say, "Zahera." English's voice is louder. Maybe they're arguing about whether tonight is the night they'll kill me or not.

Now English sounds pleading. I know he's been keeping me alive and he has his reasons. What I don't know is exactly what those reasons are. Maybe he likes having someone to torture. The television is on down the hall, some news program again, CNN or something. Just now, they were quiet, listening. Then they start to cheer and chant.

"Allu Akbar! Allu Akbar!"

The chills over take me. I flop onto the bed. I'm too restless to sleep, wishing I'd been more careful, talked less and made fewer confessions.

❖

Annie said seeing signs in real life meant I was becoming more aware. I made notes in my journal of anything symbolic:

When I sleep well, in the morning I find feathers on the floor near my bed. When I have a bad vision, I lose earrings, break jewelry or my watch stops working. When I question if I'm doing the right thing, I see symbols, rainbows or crosses in windows. Sometimes I see a shadowy shape cast on something. The light bulbs in my apartment blow out on a regular basis. I have to buy them in bulk. Sometimes when I look at the digital clock, I notice all of the numbers lined up like five fifty-five or three thirty-three. I bless myself and pray whenever this happens. I don't know why I do it. It's just instinct. Since I had no luck figuring out what the symbols meant, I called Annie.

"What do you think it all means?" I asked.

"Spirits feed on energy and electricity," she said. "I wouldn't worry too much about it. Seeing symbols is a good sign. It means your guides are helping you. I might have to research the feathers. I remember reading a story once about an angel who fell in love with a mortal. The angel fought a demon for the man's soul, but she lost so many of her beautiful feathers in the process that she fell from grace. It was a fable about the ultimate sacrifice. I don't know if that helps or not."

"It's a nice story Annie, but I don't attract angelic types."

"Maybe your luck will change, Janice."

"I guess anything is possible."

"The jewelry seems like a warning of some kind. Perhaps it's to make you aware of something, a sign of caution."

"Of what?" I asked.

"Again, I can't be certain. Are you sure there's nothing else?"

"If there is, I'm too tired or too busy to notice it."

"The watches and the numbers are both about time. I believe these signs refer to something else. You're not seeing the connection. Perhaps this is a request or a call to action."

"What kind of action?" I asked.

"Like I said, you're new at this, so you're most likely overlooking something. Remember, my messages are usually about water. Sometimes I see something on the bay. I might see the name of a boat or a pattern on the surface. You are always watching the clock, so maybe that's how they try to communicate. They know you'll get the message, eventually."

But I wasn't getting it. I'd had so much trouble with watches I'd started relying on the digital kind. The digital alarm clock in my room was the only dependable timepiece I had left. Then it went berserk.

The first number disappeared completely, and the second number was stuck in the shape of a J. The other numbers still worked perfectly fine, but if I didn't know the hour, I was lost. I plugged it in and out, but nothing changed. Even though the alarm still worked, the darned clock was driving me crazy.

I overslept one Sunday and was late meeting Gram for Mass.

"Janice, God only asks for an hour of your time every week. You owe him the full hour," she whispered.

I didn't see any point in trying to explain myself. I wanted to say that I was already giving more hours than most, but she wouldn't have understood me. I stared down at my hymnal, studying the words on the page and not looking at the visiting priest, who was filling in for Father B.

In his homily he said, "What does the Lord ask of us? How do we answer his call?" My eyes glazed over while he read a passage from Job 9:16. "If I had called and he had answered me, yet would I not believe that he had hearkened unto my voice?"

Faith was a mystery that a lost soul like me could never hope to solve.

❖

After Mass, I took Gram to our weekly haunt, The Bayside Diner, which was really a small family style restaurant. The food was good, plentiful, and inexpensive. Sue Hall, the owner, made all of the muffins and pies herself. She had a secret ingredient in her blueberry pancakes that I figured out was cornmeal. I called her out on it, but she flat-out denied it.

If I had to describe Sue, I'd say she was plump and had a pretty face framed in an unnaturally red hairdo, like a waitress from the 1950's. Maybe she'd never changed since then. Sue was divorced. Most people knew it was best to avoid bringing up any subject involving men, marriage, divorce, or romance of any kind. If anyone made that mistake, she'd get all weepy and emotional. Then the whole place would go to rack and ruin and nobody would get breakfast. North Beach can be a melancholy place.

Everyone had a story and most didn't end well. People in our town were stuck in a time warp; they stayed in the seventies or the eighties while the rest of us had moved on. I kid you not. I saw a mullet hairstyle almost every day. Worse than that were the women walking around in peg-leg jeans, popular twenty-five years ago. I hadn't yet seen a pair that flattered, because even the smallest behind looked bigger in those. In a way, it was a shame jeans were so darn sturdy because if not, people would have bought more stylish pairs every few years.

Sue was having one of her moments. I tried to console her and told her how she made the best darn pancakes in all of Maryland. Lucky for us, we had already ordered when things fell apart. Some dummy up at the counter had said something about seeing Sue's ex, Billy Hall, on a fishing trip. Sue totally lost it.

From the direction of the kitchen, I heard glass shattering. Gram shook her head. Having handled her own divorce with such dignity, she had precious little patience for Sue's antics. We ate fast and left shortly after.

I dropped Gram at her front door, and watched her walk up the path. She looked older somehow and hunched over. When did she get so old? Why hadn't I noticed it before? I was already home when I realized she'd left her bible in the pocket of my car door. I brought it up to my apartment and wondered if she'd forgotten it on purpose.

CHAPTER FOURTEEN
Guillotine

Thou shalt tread upon the lion and adder: the young lion and the dragon shalt thou trample under feet. —Psalm 91:13, KJV

English leaves the door open. He's listening to Mozart with the volume on high. Since I suspect they all understand me, I ask, "Why are you the only one who ever talks to me?"

"The others only speak the language of the infidels when it is unavoidable."

I'm seeing him differently now; filtering everything he says through a stiff veil of hatred.

"So?" he says. "What did you think of the photographs? Interesting, wouldn't you say?"

I press my lips together, making the closest thing to a seal. I refuse to give him anything and because a new odor is taking over the room. I want to seal my nose too, because I know Bo is here somewhere. I start shaking and wish I could will myself to stop. It's warmer in the room than usual. But I'm not sure if it's the room or me. Bo babbles something to English.

"Who else did you tell about the tunnel?" English asks me.

He wants to play interrogator and captive again. Fuck him.

"I didn't tell anyone," I say

"That is," he says, "a lie."

He's right.

I feel a sharp pinch. Terrible pain shoots down the length of my arm. Hot blood trickles to my wrist. Bo shows some skill with a knife. After all, English is just another mouthpiece.

"We will make you bleed slowly like a sheep. We will give you a thousand cuts, if necessary. Every time you lie, you will bleed."

The warm room and the smell make me woozy. *Please, God. Help me out here. I'm dead. I'm dead. I'm dead.* I start babbling. "The messages just come to me. I don't ask for them. I didn't mean to wreck your plan. It was an accident."

Bo says something to English in fast, short sentences. He's pissed off. They keep talking. I perk up like a dog when I hear Za-hera, the name they use for me instead of my Christian name.

I also hear Hassan and Ahmed again, and again. Bo yells something about me as he leaves. The only English words he uses are *American* and *whore*. He has me pegged. I can't deny those accusations.

"Sadly, Janice, your life has so little value that you might, in fact, be useless to us. I have tried to spare you, but I am running out of reasons. We will succeed with or without your assistance."

He goes on. "No one misses you Zahera. Even if anyone cared about your disappearance, you would still be a worthless girl. Who would even pay ransom for you? What evidence have you shown of the abilities that you claim to have? It pains me to know I have argued to extend your life. How I have put myself in this precarious position, when you continue to disappoint me."

"Can you tell me something?" I ask.

"I don't see why I should take questions from you," he snaps.

"I will help you, but I don't know what you want," I say.

"What is your question?" He asks.

"What does Zahera mean?"

"Za-hera. Clever girl. I'll get to that. First, I want to tell you something. Yesterday, I met your friend, Mrs. Sivkulanitz. She is a very fragile person, isn't she? It is a shame such a frail lady lives all alone. A lady like her could easily slip and fall down the long staircase in your apartment building."

I make an effort to sound sincere. I feel like stabbing him with the fork. "I want to help you. Just tell me what you need to know."

"I believe that you desire to help your friends," he says. "I'm not convinced that you wish to help me. I need to know the fate of our next operation, Janice. If you know the unknown, prove it and save everyone you love. If you are a liar, we will simply kill you all. Oh and Za-hera means witch. Time is up, Janice. Consult with your God."

I prayed but not for what he wanted. I asked God to end my life. I prayed he would sacrifice me to save my friends.

❖

Life drifted back to normal for a spell. I knew now not to take that for granted. For months, I'd been socking away my second paycheck and building a small fortune in my bank account. I still clung to the hope I might one day go to college. The premonitions became routine. The spirits told me something. I'd thank them for the tip, jot it down in my journal and then move on.

By early April, my belly was popping out and I knew I was going to have to start making some serious confessions. At work, I walked around with a box of doughnuts so everyone would think I was just getting super fat.

The whole process of pregnancy blew my mind. I followed the stages and knew just what was happening inside my body. Jessie was sprouting eyebrows and eyelids. It was fascinating to think my slight frame could grow another human being.

Working with Stefania was a welcome relief from the other aspects of my life where I felt like a big, fat liar. Clair was out most of time, leaving me the chance to talk to Stefania about babies and life. When I'd ask about Francesco, she wouldn't seem to notice I was interested in him. She would go on about her whole family. I loved that escape into her world, so much more interesting than mine.

I wanted to tell her about the psychic stuff, but I still wasn't sure how she'd react. It could be a touchy subject. Cilla just wasn't getting it. I found it frustrating how biased she was toward science. Annie was the only one left for me to talk to and was probably the best person to help me sort through things. I only hoped I wasn't being a complete pest.

Between my covert pregnancy and my newfound psychic capability, I felt like some kind of secret agent. Only instead of the government, I was working for the angels. I was a secret agent of God. I imagined he was disappointed with my job performance so far. I wasn't what you'd call a quick study.

❖

I woke up again at J o'clock, better known as 3:00 a.m. and stared at the red glowing digits. Annie was right I was obsessed with time. People tell insomniacs not to do this, but it's all we ever do. I guessed it was anxiety. It was time for me to tell the world some of my secrets. I had no foreknowledge of the outcome. I kept watching the numbers. I kept waiting for them to talk to me.

At J:08 I considered just giving in and getting up. There was something about this time. As a kid, I used to make words out of the numbers on a calculator and show them to my friends in math class. The numbers seven, seven, three and four, when you turned the calculator upside down spelled hell.

I looked at the clock again. J08 spelled *JOB*. I switched on the light and searched for Gram's bible, trying to remember the other numbers I had noticed on my clock over the last few days. I'd seen 8:16 a.m., 9:20 p.m., and 10:22 p.m. I flipped through the bible pages of the book of Job and read the passages that corresponded to each of these times.

Job 10:22 said, "A land of darkness, as darkness itself; and the shadow of death, without any order, and where the light is as darkness."

Shoot. God wanted me to read the bible. That was the message. Everything he needed to tell me was already in one book. I made notes in my journal until I was too exhausted to see straight.

When I woke up on the following morning, Gram's bible was in the bed next to me. The clock showed that it was 6:15 a.m. The J had vanished and the numbers on the digital screen were back to normal. Somehow, the clock had repaired itself while I slept.

❖

The door opens with a bang. Bo and his odor return. With his dragon breath, he is yelling something foreign in my face. English translates.

"Are you with the Jinn? Are you a sorceress or a witch?"

I try to sound sure about myself. "No, I receive these messages against my will. An angel or a spiritual being tells me about the future."

"Does this spiritual being ever tell you to do harm?"

"No," I say. "Never."

"How can you be certain it is not a demon who speaks to you? Do you ask questions of it? How does it answer you? Who hears it besides you?"

"It's not something you hear with your ears. It tells me the answers in my head. It speaks through thought."

This feels like the final interview for a job where if I'm not hired, I'm getting the guillotine. They discuss what I said and English says,

"You will swear allegiance to our jihad and to the Brotherhood Against America."

The Brotherhood Against America? Was BAA the best they could do?

"Your old life is gone, Janice. Your friends no longer care about you. No one searches for you. Janice Morrison is dead. Denounce your faith. Forget your God. If you lie, it will be at the expense of your own tongue. If you refuse to help us, your friends will suffer painful deaths. If you dare to mislead us, we'll bring your baby here and kill it slowly before we will kill you. Have I explained everything clearly?"

I nod, keeping my mouth closed and my tongue safe.

"I have faith in you, Janice," English says, stroking my cheek with his hand. "I know that you won't displease me."

He leaves me and the room seems instantly darker. Faces flash across my mind. I see Jessie, Stefania, Cilla, Ken, Mrs. S., and Bridge. Am I too late? Will they suffer horrible deaths because of me? Will they die because they are my friends? It's not enough to escape. Now I want to hurt these men. Could it be true no one is looking for me anymore?

No. He lies. I've heard the news. People are searching for me. At least, people were searching for me. If anyone is going to find me, I'll need to send a sign. *God, angels, or whoever speaks to me, please don't quit on me now.*

English says I must denounce my faith and swear allegiance to the BAA. If I only pretend to do this, is it still a sin? Probably. If I stop calling God by name and I call him something else for a spell, will he mind? Will he strike me down? If Bo cuts off my head, will I go to hell? Is anything worse than being headless in hell? Is there a hell? Am I already there?

Will it even matter if I help them? Either way, my soul is damned. Jihads are not good things. I've heard about holy wars on the news. I've heard about people killing Americans in the name of God, but they're wrong. I read about Muhammad. He was a prophet. You can twist the ancient words. As with the bible, you can interpret the words incorrectly. Nonbelievers say that there are passages about violence and about an angry God who strikes out at people. There are more passages about a forgiving God.

I can't wrap my brain around killing in the name of religion. From what I've read, though, people have been fighting about it forever, even though most of us share the same beliefs. This is crazy. What if we are all worshiping the same God and calling him different names? Is it worth killing one another over a name? I know God doesn't approve of murder, no matter what we call him.

I hear muffled voices and a car engine outside of the house. Someone leaves but someone else is still working in the kitchen, banging pots and pans. After some time, English walks down the hall. Through the door, he says, "Knock on the wall if you need to use the facilities."

All I need to do is knock. I have the fork and enough hatred to fuel my strength. I could wedge the fork into his neck, but I don't. I have something else in mind for the fork.

CHAPTER FIFTEEN
Synchronicity

There shall no evil befall thee, neither shall plague come nigh thy dwelling. For he shall give his angels charge over thee, to keep thee in all thy ways. —Psalm 91:10–11, KJV

Without Bo around, English is gentle again. I ignore the way he's acting. It's just another trick. I keep my loathing fresh and close to the surface. Today, I get to take a shower.

"I'm pleased you have decided to join our mission so willingly. Since you know the risks now, I trust that you will not try anything stupid." He unties my hands.

"What if I do?" I foolishly bait him.

With his matter-of-fact tone, he puts me in my place. "Then my brother will gauge out your eyes."

He leads me down the hall. "Oh, I almost forgot. Your friend, Mrs. Sivkulanitz, is in a nursing home. I thought that you should know. It seems she took a nasty fall and broke her hip. It's a very sad situation in that it's difficult to recover from serious injuries at her age. I'm sure you know all about these things."

Frozen in anger and fear, I'm standing inside the bathroom doorway when he shuts the door in my face. I do as I'm told. Obedience is a virtue I cling to for survival.

It takes a couple of seconds for the water to heat up. I peer out of the gap in the black paper. The house next door is at some distance behind the trees. I have yet to see any signs of life over there. Now that the leaves have fallen, a realtor sign is visible through the trees. The yard is overgrown. Maybe someone will move in soon enough to help me. I pray for my new potential neighbors who will help me escape. They just don't know it yet.

❖

Where is my journal? I'm thinking about what I wrote the day after I went through the tunnel and about all of my predictions and their outcomes. If I find my way out of this cell, I might yet land myself in a padded one.

I always keep my journal in my pocketbook. On the day of the kidnapping, I left it in the car. I was running late from Safe Harbor, and walking toward the rectory to get Jessie. I've tried to forget her. This sounds awful, but thinking about her makes me ache inside. One way or another, I'll die and she'll be motherless. It's best for me to let go. On the day they captured me, all I had on me were my keys. Surely, someone has gone through my car by now. Do the sisters of Mercy have my journal? Do the police have it? Neither of these are good options.

❖

Annie had told me to stop in anytime. People always said this sort of thing, though most didn't mean it. Annie was an exception to all rules. With her back facing me, she was outside cleaning and painting her sailboat, which was dry-docked in the driveway.

"I'll be right down, Janice. Don't risk climbing the ladder."

Misty rain settled on everything. It was damp enough to be annoying and not a great day for painting. The sun peered around a cloud. Annie climbed down the ladder with a wet brush in her hand. She stuck it in a can of some kind of strong smelling liquid.

"It's great to see you. You barely look any different. How's the pregnancy?" she asked.

"Good." Ever since Cilla knew that I was pregnant, I'd gone from being eager to talk about it to being tired of talking about it. Cilla was driving me crazy. She kept asking me when I'd tell everybody, more for her own benefit than mine, since she said she'd burst if she had to keep quiet much longer. Cilla's latest quest was to meet Annie. I wasn't keen on setting that meeting up.

Annie was easier to be around and not one to pressure people. We walked to the backyard and sat in the Adirondack chairs. White paint was all over her clothes and she even had flecks of it in her hair. "I love painting, but I should leave it to the pros. I get more on myself than I do the boat," she said.

The sun behind her cast a glowing outline around her body. Out on the bay, a faint spray of pastel colors arched over the water.

"Well, that's a good sign," she said, smiling.

"I still don't know how you know what's a sign and what's just your imagination."

"You don't see the rainbow?"

"Sure, I see it. Shoot, Annie. I see rainbows everywhere now. I see them in puddles, on road signs, and on bumper stickers. So what?"

Before all of this, I hadn't put much thought into signs. Now that I was a regular at the library, I was getting an education in the paranormal. On one of my trips to the library, I saw a book sitting on the reference desk about symbols. I tucked it into my checkout pile. The librarian asked how my project was going. She was on to me. I'm sure she saw liars like me every day.

Rainbows symbolize redemption, good news, or forgiveness. They're associated with a quest for self-knowledge and thought to be the bridge between heaven and earth, a pathway toward an enlightened mind. I wasn't feeling very enlightened. I was feeling overwhelmed and confused.

"Signs and symbols are always there," Annie said, "waiting for us to notice them. This is how the spirit world seeks to get our attention. When you acknowledge and interpret them in real time—not just in dreams—you cross over a boundary, Janice."

You cross right into the land of no return.

"Synchronicity," she said, referring to one of Carl Jung's theories. In this theory, an unconscious image comes into consciousness either directly or indirectly. It comes through a dream, an idea, or a premonition, and it coincides with a real situation. In other words, when you see something happen in your mind, sometimes it happens in the real world too.

"Spiritually, you've traveled a long distance in a short amount of time," she said.

"Is it too late to turn back then?"

"Why?"

"To be normal again," I said.

"Everyone has a different sense of what is normal, Janice. This is what will become normal to you."

Edgar Cayce, the famous sleeping psychic, said that people would someday realize that everyone has psychic abilities. He planned to return in the year 2100. The world will be a much different place then. I wondered if he could come back just a little sooner.

❖

Stefania had to bring Aunt Maria and Uncle Enzo to the airport. They were flying to New York for a bit before going home to Italy. Worried about being alone in Baltimore at night, Stefania asked me to go with her. Girls like us always have to think about things men take for granted, like personal safety. Francesco was supposed to take them to the airport. Instead, he'd gone out with some girl and wasn't answering his phone.

I'd met Stefania at her parents' house after work. We left immediately. A bout of April showers passed through. I'd had the shivers all day, and I couldn't shake the cold feeling in my bones. Inside, I quietly stewed about Francesco's date.

"Who's this girl he's seeing? What's she like?"

"Who knows," Stefania said. "Some *butana*."

I felt sad thinking about how Aunt Maria and Uncle Enzo were leaving. We had a nice chat on the way to BWI, and they made me promise to visit them in Naples after I had my baby. I promised, but I had no idea how I'd deliver. It occurred to me this was true on multiple levels.

After we got Maria and Enzo checked in, we said our goodbyes and watched them walk arm-in-arm through the security line. It made me feel warm inside. Would I ever find someone to love, someone to grow old with me? It was the curse of the Morrison women to wind up alone.

Stefania and I went back to the car. Once we settled in, she locked eyes with me and said, "Claire knows."

"What? What do you mean? How?"

"Wait. It's worse," she said, putting her hand on my arm. "Janice, I worry about you. I saw her looking at you yesterday. Later, I heard her talking to Jason on the telephone. When she and Mr. Dick went to bed, I made pretend to go to my room. Instead, I sneak down the hall and listen at the door."

"Crap! What did they say?"

"She blames you, of course. She's going to Safe Harbor on Friday to tell Mel everything. She wants more than to fire you. I think she wants you fired from both jobs."

"Oh, God. I'm ill."

"No," Stefania said. "Listen. Dick said, 'How do we know it isn't just like the last time?' Then Claire just went crazy. She said that the girl was a big liar. She said Jason was innocent and nothing ever happened. Blah. Blah. Blah. But if so, why does Dick bring it up?"

"Stefania, you need to find out for me! Why is she waiting until Friday?"

"Are you kidding me? This is Claire. She said she won't change her plans this week. Then, she said, she wants to sue your boss, but Dick said no way, because Mel is his friend from years ago and it is not her fault. After that, they argued about Nanny and Jason, so I went to bed."

"I'm screwed," I said.

"You know something? The way Dick talks about your boss, I wonder about her."

"What do mean?"

"Well, he would not even listen when Claire said to sue your boss. You have to know about his affairs, his mistresses."

"No. I didn't know that," I said. "This is news to me."

For someone as worldly as I claim to be, I could be the most naïve person on the planet. The situation was so logical. Claire was an ice princess. I couldn't imagine Claire and Dick getting it on without Dick's penis falling off from frostbite.

"Do you really think Dick is sleeping with Mel?" I asked.

I couldn't picture that either. I always had Mel pegged for a lesbian. Go figure. This did explain a few things, though. For a split second, I almost felt sorry for Claire. Then I came back to my senses.

"He's been seeing someone anyway," she said. "The way he talks to this other woman, he knows her a long time. Claire was out Monday. I think Dick didn't know I was there. It's usually my market day. When he came down the stairs, he was talking on his phone. His voice was different, soft and sweet. It's all business with Claire, you know. When he walked into the kitchen and saw me, he looked very nervous. I just smiled and said, 'Buon giorno, Mr. Dick. Are you hungry?' I made like I didn't hear a thing."

"I hope you're right," I said. "If they sue Mel, it will be all my fault. I have to get to Mel before Claire does. Thanks for telling me."

"Listen Janeeze, if you lose your job and have no place to go, my family would love to take you and your new baby."

"Thanks, Stefania, but I still have Gram. Oh, crap! Thanks to Claire, I have to tell Gram right away that I'm pregnant. Claire, that—"

"I know what you mean," Stefania said. "That *straga*."

"What's a *straga*?"

"It's a witch. But it's too good of a word for her. There's another word, but I cannot use it."

"Stefania, pray for me."

"Always." She held the wheel with her thigh and made the motion of the praying hands. "You need it."

"Don't I know it?"

Neither one of us knew our way around the northern part of Maryland. Since we were talking instead of paying attention, we went the wrong way on the highway and got lost. Somehow, we ended up going through the Baltimore Harbor Tunnel, which was nowhere near the airport.

I'm not sure if it was my anxiety about knowing that my life was over or if it was fate's idea to kick a person when she was down so low she could hardly see which way was up. Things took a bad turn. Passing through the tunnel, I felt like I was in a well of liquid unhappiness. A sense of terror descended on me. Then, I saw the biggest mental photo album I'd ever seen. Hundreds of faces were flying at me. I screamed.

"Stefania, pull over!"

When we were outside of the tunnel, she pulled off to the side of the road. Cars honked and screeched all around us. I jumped out of the car and vomited with vengeance into the drainage ditch. Within seconds, Stefania was standing next to me.

"I'm so sorry. I upset you. I thought you'd want to know."

"I can't breathe," I said and gulped at the air like a fish on dry land. I braced myself with my hands on my knees. The world was spinning. When I finally caught my breath, we climbed back into the car. Stefania handed me a tissue and merged back into the flow of traffic.

"I'm so sorry," she said.

"No, it's not Claire. Stefania, do you believe God sends us messages?"

"Si, messaggi inviato da Dio—sent by God." She said this calmly, as if it were no big deal. "Why?"

"Well, he just sent me a doozy."

When I explained what had been happening to me, Stefania took it better than I'd expected.

"Janeeze, you must tell someone about this tunnel problem right away. What if something happens? What if the tunnel falls down? What if you can save these people? Do you want this on your head?"

"Stefania, I don't have anything specific to tell. Right now, I don't know why, how or when something will happen or even who is responsible. I just know it's coming. What would I say? I can't call the cops and say what I've just said to you. They'll think I'm a lunatic."

"I don't know," she said. "You must find a way. It is your responsibility now."

That wasn't what I'd wanted to hear. We stopped at a gas station to ask for directions. On the way back home, I told Stefania about the journal and the rest of my story. By the time she dropped me at my car, I was drained and exhausted. In the drizzle and chill, she said, "I wish I could help you, but the message came to you for a reason."

This is the notion I thought about as I drove away. It was up to me to find a way to stop the carnage in the tunnel, only I had no idea how.

CHAPTER SIXTEEN
Coincidence

I hope Mrs. S. will be OK. I say a prayer for her. Of everyone I am close to, Annie is the second oldest. She will be next on their list. Would she be able to see it coming? Without saying a word, English walks in, switches on the light, and sits in the chair. He's flipping through the pages of a book. "This is such a fascinating little story. Shall I read some of it to you?"

"Sure," I say. "Read away."

"Watch your tone, Janice. Ahmed is only a phone call away. Although I am struggling to believe you, he does not."

If Bo is Ahmed and Ape is Saif, then, English is Hassan. The other man, Chief aka Muhammad, has not been back. I prefer the names I've secretly given them.

"I'm sorry," I say. "Hassan."

"Oh." He laughs. "So, you're a little linguist now. You see, I was right again. I knew you were a smart girl. I like it when you surprise me, Janice. It makes me want to keep you alive for longer. Let me see. There are so many good parts here. It is hard to know where to begin. Ah, here is something pertinent:

'When I told Stefania I'd go with her to the airport, who knew I'd have the worst premonition of them all on that day.'

Shall I continue? Hmm. I like the looks of that girl, Stefania. She is so beautiful and vivacious like a wild Arabian Mare. A man could ride her until she breaks. No, don't try to get up, Janice. You'll force me to do something you'll later regret. This book of yours appears to support your claims. For all I know, though, it could just be the ravings of a lunatic."

I'm the lunatic here. Really?

❖

I couldn't call Mel to break the news. I had to meet with her face to face. It had to wait until after work on Thursday.

My problems had finally bubbled over to a point where I couldn't handle them on my own. Between my angst over the tunnel and my soon-to-be unemployed ass, I needed help. I made notes for my meeting with Father Ballentine. I'd known him for most of my life and figured he knew I wasn't crazy. His knowledge of my family history was a bonus. I hoped he might offer a logical explanation of my psychic predicament, like depression. Maybe he wouldn't think it was odd that God was sending me text messages from heaven.

After an hour of stewing in my own juice, I did one of Annie's clearing exercises and I said a prayer. I was trying to cover all of my bases before I fell into a dead sleep. There were no more flying faces that night.

The next day, my butt was still dragging. The pregnancy was wearing my body out. I put a good face on and pretended not to know about Claire's evil plan. It was harder than I thought, since she was nastier than she normally behaved. I caught her staring at me more than once. I fought the urge to tell her to stuff it.

Before I left for the day, Nanny was awake and alert. I said my piece, not knowing if I'd get another chance. I didn't want her to think I'd quit, so I told her the whole truth about Jason and me. Out of respect, I made him out to be better than he was. She loved him, after all. Of course, I didn't hold back from explaining everything about Claire. I figured we were on the same page. It felt good to get it all off my chest.

"Guess what, Nanny? You're going to be a great-grandmother. Jason's the Dad. Don't worry, though. It won't mess up his career. I'm more than capable of raising a baby on my own. Claire plans to fire me because of it, so I won't likely get to see you anymore after tomorrow. I really enjoyed taking care of you, and I hope you get better soon."

A tear formed in the corner of her good eye. She squeezed my hand. For a moment, I let myself think that she might get better. I wouldn't see her again. I was going to miss her. I left the O'Neil home and sped to Safe Harbor. Mel was in her office. She looked up from her paperwork and put her glasses on.

"Man, you are porking out, Janice. You better lay off the sweets."

"Mel, I'm pregnant."

"Holy hell!" she said, slamming her pen down on the desk.

"I know," I said. "It gets worse."

"I can't imagine how?"

She put her head in her hands.

"The baby is Jason O'Neil's."

"Jesus H. Christ!" She leapt up and threw her hands in the air. "Damn it, Janice! I thought you were a smart kid?" She was pacing around her office. Then she pointed at me. "I handpicked you for that assignment!"

"I couldn't be sorrier, Mel. I know I've let you down."

"Damn it! Do they know yet?"

"I'm afraid Claire has an inkling."

"No wonder she wants to see me tomorrow! Goddamn it! Do you think I really need to get my ass reamed by that bitch?"

"Mel, I'm so sorry! Believe me! Do you think I want to be in this condition?" I pleaded, gesturing toward my stomach. "He jumped me! Rumor has it, the kid's a rapist and he's done this before."

"How do you know this?" Mel asked, crossing her arms. "Fuck me! I need a drink." She reached into her desk drawer, uncapped a flask, and took a slug out of it.

"I'm friends with the cook. She heard the whole story."

"Is she an illegal?" Mel asked, taking another long draw on her small metal flask.

"No. She's a US Citizen. She's Italian, for crying out loud." I don't know where I thought I was going with that.

"What am I going to do with you, Janice? Oh, great! What am I supposed to do when you're out on maternity leave? Who's going to do your job?"

"You mean I'm not fired?" I asked, feeling hopeful for the first time.

"You're certainly fired from the O'Neil job, but I still need you here. Dammit, Janice. You're killing me!" she said, pounding her forehead with a closed fist.

"I think Claire wants me fired from here as well."

"That's not her decision to make. You let me handle Claire. This is going to be a mess for you. Have you thought about that?"

"For what it's worth, I never meant for this to happen. How do you think I feel? I'm having a baby for cripes sake. Don't you think I'm scared shitless?"

I started to cry. I wasn't usually a crier. It was the damn hormones.

"OK," Mel said. "Quit balling. You know I hate that shit," Handing me a tissue, she said, "OK, here's the plan. Tomorrow, as per usual, you will report to the O'Neil house. You will act as though everything is normal and we never had this conversation. See what your maid friend can dig up on the O'Neil kid. You don't know what Claire is capable of doing. I may need some ammunition. It's a good thing Dick and I have known each other since high school."

"Mel, I'm telling you the truth. The kid's an animal."

"I wish that mattered, Janice. I have to call Dick. Try and find out the name of the other girl. The problem is, Janice, these people have money and a reputation to protect. This thing won't end with firing you as their personal nurse's aid. It's much messier than that. Let me get through my meeting with Claire tomorrow. I want to see where she's going with this. Jesus, Janice. You're a pain in my fucking ass!"

"I know that, Mel. Thank you for not firing me."

She waved me out of her office. "Go! Go do your job before I change my mind. And for Christ's sake no more problems! Don't let me hear any gripping about swollen ankles or sore backs or I will fire you." Pointing at the door with her pen, she added, "Close my door behind you."

At dinner, I told Cilla what had happened, blow by blow. I even wound up telling her my premonition about the tunnel. Confessing was an old habit I guess I couldn't break. She was so engrossed in my baby drama she didn't seem to pay any attention to the rest of what I'd told her. I swore her to secrecy again and she crossed her heart, saying it was all in the vault.

Cilla promised to rearrange her patient schedule the next morning. She planned to post herself outside of Mel's office during the meeting with Claire and promised she'd call me immediately with an update.

When I arrived at the O'Neil house the following morning, there was no sign of Claire. According to the calendar, she had a hair appointment. I went about my day being so distracted I nearly forgot all about Nanny's lunch. It felt like a funeral. Disgusted with Claire, Stefania kept shaking her head and threatening to quit.

"You need to keep your job in order to save up for your business. Don't worry about me. I'm like a cat. I always land on my feet," I said.

After the meal cleanup, I felt my cell phone vibrate in my pocket. While Nanny napped, I slipped out into the hall to take the call.

"Oh, my God!" Cilla whispered into the phone.

I wanted to tell her God didn't appreciate people using his name in vain, but it just wasn't the right time.

"Cilla, where are you? I can barely hear you."

"I'm in Mrs. Brown's room. She's napping and mostly deaf anyway. I've never seen Mel so mad. It was a real catfight. She actually stood up for you, you know."

"Cilla, where is Claire now?

"She stormed out of here about five minutes ago. I wanted to warn you."

"I'll be long gone by the time she gets back. Thanks, Cilla."

"Don't mention it. Just hurry. I want to tell you the rest."

I had about fifteen minutes to get the heck out of there. I hugged Stefania good-bye. I knew we'd still be friends, but I was going to miss working with her every day. Stefania promised to do her best to make life miserable for Claire and then gave me a going-away present.

"I copied something for you that I found in Mr. Dick's desk. It was from his lawyer," she said.

The document contained the name of a girl who left Georgetown after a reported rape. Jason was the accused perpetrator of this crime. He had attacked the girl but nothing had come of the allegations. Both parties had agreed to a settlement. I wanted to call the girl myself, but I knew that this might have made things worse.

"Stefania I owe you one," I said.

I gave Francis a scratch on the head on my way out. He cocked his head sideways and whimpered. Then he put his head down on his paws. I swear all animals have a sixth sense.

My firing was a kind of blessing. Exhaustion was my permanent state, and I didn't want to risk running into Jason again.

When I got to Safe Harbor, Mel said, "I fixed your problem—for now, anyway. Your replacement starts on Monday. I convinced Claire you wouldn't make any trouble. Don't make a liar out of me."

"Thanks, Mel," I said. "I owe you."

She shook her head. "I always thought you were a smart kid, Janice."

❖

Later that night, I did something else stupid. I was online shopping baby store websites and checking messages when I saw Ken was online. I started chatting with him:

"HRU & Cilla doing?"
"GR8! THNX again."
"BTW, at work, do U investigate peeps who blow things up?"
"Yes, why? What things?"
"Like tunnels."
"Why?"
"No reason. Who would?"
"What?"
"Blow up a tunnel?"
"Terrorists."
"OK. We don't have them in MD, right?"
"Janice, did U C something?"
"No, just watching the news."
"If U did C something, U need to say something."
"OK. Sure thing."
"And yes, we have terrorists here and everywhere."
"OK. GNITE."
"U worry me, Janice."
"Relax."

❖

Ken was easy to chat with, even if I did feel worse after hearing about the terrorists, I slept better knowing smart folks like Ken were on the good guys side. How was I supposed to know that long before our little chat he already knew much more than he let on? How could I have known that he and Cilla would unintentionally help put my ass in a whopper of a sling?

❖

I had to tell Gram about the baby. I felt like a total heel. She was, after all, my only family member. It wasn't fair for her to be the last one to learn about my status. Instead of focusing on my work, this was what I was thinking.

My patient swap with Cilla was working out just fine. I gave Mr. Bates a hard time about his indecent behavior, and he ignored me and watched the news on the small TV that jutted out of the corner of the wall.

After I gathered up his lunch tray, I immediately dropped it, making a terrible mess. If I'd been in Mr. Jameson's room when this happened, I'd be getting another write-up. While I cleaned up, Mr. Bates just snickered at me.

The anchorman on the TV said, "During rush hour yesterday, Baltimore police shot and killed a man who was attempting to enter the Baltimore Harbor Tunnel with a bomb in his van. The alleged suspect, Bashshar Karim Al-Aziz, was transporting an ammonium nitrate-fuel oil bomb, better known as an ANFO bomb. Sources say based on an ongoing investigation, federal agents were conducting routine searches of all vans and cargo trucks entering the tunnel. The suspect rammed a police barricade and began firing a gun at nearby officers. Wounded by return gunfire, Al-Aziz died at the scene. The bomb squad was able to control and dismantle the bomb and avoid any further casualties. It is unknown if Al-Aziz has connections to Al Qaeda or if he may be part of a home grown terror cell operating in the Baltimore area."

Mr. Bates was talking to me, but I didn't hear anything he said.

"Sorry, Mr. Bates, I'll get this cleaned up."

"In my day, we didn't have any of this baloney—all this sneaking around. You knew who your enemies were."

"Right," I said.

Sometimes your enemies were even your closest friends. I tracked Cilla down by the vending machines. She was stuffing a candy bar into her mouth.

"So much for the diet," I barked.

"Well, that was mean," she said with chocolate dribbling down her chin. As she wiped it, she looked like she might start to cry.

"It's not as mean as telling secrets that you swore that you'd keep. That's some vault you have. It's more like a leaky faucet."

"What happened?" she said, sounding cagey.

"What did you tell Ken about the tunnel?"

"Oh."

"Oh," I said. "That's all you have to say? You promised me, Cilla! People are only as good as their promises, and yours are unreliable." It was something Gram would have said. I needed Cilla to feel some of my pain.

"I'm sorry, Janice," she said. "It's just that I'm worried about you. I needed to talk to someone."

"You needed to talk to someone? What about me? Does anyone care about what I need?" I left her standing there holding her empty candy wrapper.

I called Ken that night. If he was involved in capturing the bomber, it was a good thing. What I was upset about was Cilla's gossiping. Only I had the right to tell my secrets, me and no one else.

Almost immediately, Ken admitted that Cilla had spilled the beans, but he said that he didn't believe in psychics. He swore he'd never said anything to anybody. I knew that the CIA paid people to be professional liars among other things. People like Ken. According to Ken, the story wasn't even big news. He said, foiled terrorist attempts were common and most never even made the news. It could have been a coincidence, I guessed. I could have put it out of my mind. Except that, I no longer believed in coincidences.

CHAPTER SEVENTEEN
Auxiliary

He shall call upon me, and I will answer him: I will be with him in trouble; I will deliver him and honour him. With long life will I satisfy him, and shew him my salvation. —Psalm 91:15–16, KJV

I hear music and I start to sweat until I know it isn't classical but rock music. Hassan is on the phone making plans and I begin to work on mine. As far as he knows, I'm behaving, so he keeps my hands free.

I bend the fork and tuck it inside my underwear. It's practically unbearable. With my toiletries neatly stacked on top my towel, I wait for Hassan to come in for his inspection. He doesn't feed me, but allows me to shower.

Inside the bathroom, I lock the door, run the water, slip the fork out, and get right to work. The corners of the twelve-panel window will be too obvious. I choose a section halfway up and in the middle. It's a spot where the paper buckles and I can fit my hand up through it. With the fork, I work the grout. Bit by bit, it falls out from around the glass. I drop the scraps into the toilet. I don't dare do too much before I mix some toothpaste with water and use it to caulk the glass again. Dried leaves are floating by the window. If I escape, will fall ever be the same time of beauty?

I double-check my work, taking care not to leave any signs behind. I quickly shower and flush away the evidence. I unlock the door before he has a chance to try the handle. Then I put my blindfold, a constant annoyance, back in place. If I could see, I'd be able to read Hassan better.

"You need to take shorter showers," he says on our way back to my room.

I perch on the edge of the bed. "Wouldn't it be easier on you if I didn't have this blindfold? I know if I try anything, you'll hurt one of my friends. Why would I risk it? If I could see, I could feed myself and save you the trouble."

In a weird way, I think I might miss the meals I have with Hassan. It's been my only form of human contact.

"So, now you want to be little miss helpful?" he says. "Is that what I am expected to believe?"

"Yes, I do."

"I'll consider your request, but first you need to do something for me." He sets the chair in front of me. His knees brush against mine. I feel his breath on my face. All this time, I've feared he'd ask for something sexual. Maybe this was going to be it.

"Sure," I say. "What do you need?"

"It should be very easy for you. I'll show you some pictures and you'll tell me what you see."

I sigh. I'm relieved for a second until the weight of it settles. The last pictures he showed me scared the living crap out of me.

"What kind of pictures?"

"Potential targets. I want to see what sense you get from them."

"I'm not sure," I say. "I mean, I may not get any sense from just a picture. I usually have to actually go to the place, assuming it's a place we could go." I carefully cast my line without a snag.

"In the past, you saw things through the television. You learned the fate of that the reporter or so you said in your journal."

Just like that, my hook lands in the reeds, thanks to my damn journal. "Yes, that's true. I'll do my best."

"I know you will, Janice. Annie's life depends on it. The pictures are on the bed. I'll leave the light on."

❖

Gram was acting strangely. When I called her home phone, I'd get the machine. She was missing work. I meant to ask her about it, but I overslept and missed Mass the week before. I urgently needed to tell her about the baby before someone else in town did it for me. Otherwise, I'd never live it down.

Saturday morning, on my way to do see Father B., I saw Grams car in the driveway. I stopped in, determined to confess my baby news and to find out what was going on with Gram.

"Your mother called," she said.

"What?" I asked unaccustomed to hearing Dee mentioned at all especially in that context. Gram looked at me. Her face had aged ten years in the last month. Dee seemed to have the same effect on everyone.

"What does she want?" I asked.

"She wants to come for a visit."

"I hope you told her not to bother."

"I didn't," Gram said. "It's probably time for her to come."

"Well, I don't want to see her," I said. "I hope she doesn't expect a warm welcome from me."

"Janice, you might want to reconsider. She's still your family, flawed as she may be."

"Flawed? Try annihilated."

"You know, it's really my fault you have no relationship with her. I kept you away from her. I realize now that I had no right to do this."

"Gram, she's a nightmare. You said so yourself. Every time she comes here, she makes a mess of things. All this time's gone by and now she wants to visit? I have enough problems. I don't need her adding to them."

"What problems?"

Good going mouth; make way for the foot. Damn you, Dee!

"I just have a lot going on with work and everything," I said.

"You don't look well lately. Are you getting enough sleep? Are you drinking enough water? Your face is so puffy."

"I'm fine, Gram. Look, I have to go. I have a million things to do today." If I got into any deep discussions, I was going to be late for my meeting. "So, when is she coming?"

"She didn't say exactly."

"Typical," I said. "Well, thanks for the warning. I'll see you tomorrow at Mass."

❖

After Hassan left, I studied the pictures. Each one brought on different feelings. My stomach throbbed with hunger. Hassan liked to starve me into submission. I could smell the food before I smelled him.

"First, I need some answers from you Janice. Then you get some lunch. So, of all of the pictures, which one do you think is the target?"

There were photographs of five different locations: a monument, an office building, a church, an airport, and a mall.

"I saw crowds of people when I looked at each one, but…"

"But?"

"When I looked at the mall, I saw the most people and…"

"And?"

"Just flashes of things," I say. "They don't make much sense. I see a moving van in a big garage, like a parking garage. I hear music. I see a mall food court with people running and screaming. There's so much smoke. And there's fire, and broken glass."

"That's very good, Janice. It's excellent, in fact. I'm sure you're hungry. I made Arnab Mikli."

I felt like a dog rewarded for catching a stick.

"Arn-a who-a?"

Hassan laughs. It's been awhile since I've heard him laugh. It's a nice laugh for a murderer. What am I thinking? This is an all-time low for me. This monster just threatened my friend.

"Ar-nab Mik-li. It's rabbit. Do you like this?"

"You mean like Bugs Bunny?"

He laughs harder.

"I'm glad I tasted it before you told me what it was."

"You're so provincial, Janice," he says. "I find it endearing."

Somehow, everything he makes tastes good. We're laughing together now, but it's weird. In a second, he can make me feel like crap, make me think about doing violent things to him.

I have to stay focused. They'll eventually kill me. Even if I can't see this in my future, I know it's out there lurking, as patient as a slow growing cancer.

❖

I learned more over the next few months than I ever wanted to know about cancer, the hard way. It was funny. I'd been selfishly thinking I was the only one walking around with secrets before I met with Father Ballentine.

Like psychiatrists, priests are supposed to keep your secrets. I've seen movies where under pressure, they get the shrink to talk or hand over his records, but they can never get the priest to give up the goods. Sometimes the doctors even set a trap and let you walk right into it. Then they put you in a straitjacket and hauled you away.

That's when it struck me, what if some of the people who were in the psycho ward were just like me? They might not have been crazy, only a little psychic. Either way, I made it a point never to tell anyone that I heard voices. I really don't hear them anyway. I think them. Hearing and thinking are not the same things.

Priests don't even write anything down or tape-record their meetings. That's how confidential it is. Medical records find their way into the wrong hands all of the time. Confidentiality is a joke. I know that employees who are bored working the night shift at Safe Harbor go into Mel's files just to snoop. I've caught them before and I should have reported them. I really should.

Anyway, you can bet if they're doing it, that people all over the place are doing the exact same thing. That's why I decided to talk to Father Ballentine about my psychic problems. I left the idea of seeing a psychiatrist as a last resort.

I'd known Father B. for years, but I was still nervous. He'd always been kind and never been creepy, thank goodness. I'd heard the stories about the pedophiles. I was tired of people saying the church was responsible for creating those creeps. The truth was that pedophiles went looking for kids anywhere they could find them: schools, day-care centers, Boy Scouts, or foster care homes—you name it. Those sly, deceitful creatures somehow snuck by other adults unnoticed, adults who didn't protect the children. The church messed up when they covered up things. Some devils walk this earth among us, and even God couldn't cure them. Lock them up and chop it off, I say.

I wasn't sure how much I'd tell Father B. but my rationale was that he was just a man who worked for God. There was no reason for me to be anxious and furthermore there was no need to tell him about my recent sinful behavior.

Since this might have constituted a sin of omission, I added it to my already long list of prayers. At the rate I was going, I'd need to sneak over the pearly gates like an illegal alien escaping from Mexico.

Father B.'s office was off to one side of the altar in the back. I won't lie. I considered leaving. He sat at his desk working on some papers. I cleared my throat when I walked in. Once he saw me, he stood up and it was too late to run away.

"Janice, it's lovely to see you. Please have a seat."

We exchanged some pleasantries and then Father B. and I bowed our heads while he said a prayer about our meeting, "Heavenly father, please bless us with your guidance and wisdom, and help us to better understand your plan for us. Amen."

Since I'd asked for the meeting, he sat and waited patiently for me to say what I'd come to say. For starters, I asked him to promise me he wouldn't talk to Gram about our meeting.

"Of course, Janice, that goes without saying. Anything we discuss here today is confidential."

Well, you couldn't be too careful. Convinced that she'd say it was all the work of the devil, I'd dropped the idea of ever talking to Gram about my predictions. She could be a bit closed-minded sometimes and I needed answers and support, not more guilt. I shifted in my seat.

"I'm sorry. I just don't know where to start," I said.

"It's always best to start at the beginning," he said, leaning forward with his hands folded on the desk.

"Right," I said.

Without further hesitation, I explained my predicament and asked my questions. I always talked fast and furious when I was nervous, and feeling jumpy. I hoped I was making some sort of sense. It was so warm in his office that the dampness under my armpits spread to my shirt.

I pulled out my journal for support. Using the examples I'd written down, I told him about the old man in the market and the people at Safe Harbor. I said I'd just had this overwhelming sense when their numbers were up.

"Why would God tell me these things?" I asked. "Why me? Did he want me to tell the people something? Did he want me to do something about it? If so, what on earth did he want me to do?"

Father B. was quiet for a bit. I could see him thinking hard about what he wanted to say. Then he blew my mind. "Janice, it's not uncommon to ask why me when the Lord gives us a task. What you have to remember is that we are all born with wonderful gifts and abilities meant for a higher purpose. To use a recent example, when I was in Rome, I went to visit the Sistine Chapel and witnessed the amazing work of Michelangelo."

"I'm not sure I follow," I said.

"What I'm saying Janice, is that it's not for us to question why, but to accept our gifts and to show thankfulness to God."

"How would I do that?" I asked.

"Well, sometimes the best thing we can do for anyone is to pray for them—to pray for their souls. It is possible these souls carry the heavy weight of sin and unresolved issues. Someone might die suddenly, for example, and not have the opportunity for a proper confession."

"Prayer? That's it?" I said. *That's so simple. Why didn't I think of it?*

"Janice, auxiliary prayer can be very powerful. People tend to focus on more earthly matters and neglect the state of their soul. Without taking care of these sins, they cannot rightfully enter the Kingdom of God. The prayers we offer on behalf of others are very pleasing to God. Have you talked to your grandmother? She's an expert on prayer."

"No. You're right," I said. "She is an expert."

I started to think about how much actual praying I did. Mostly, I prayed when I wanted something. I was sure this approach was totally wrong. How many times had God come through for me? How many times had he answered my prayers? I had never even once, thanked him. I felt quite shitty about the whole thing.

At the same time, I'd never been so relieved. Father B. was a truly nice man. You know, he didn't seem surprised or anything about what I was telling him. Maybe what I was experiencing wasn't as unusual as I thought it was. I was still reasonably normal, well paranormally.

"Janice, did you have any other questions or concerns?"

"Well, I'm having some trouble with electronic things acting haywire. My watches just stop working, even when they have new batteries. I'm having problems with jewelry just snapping and breaking while I'm wearing it. Could this be related to the visions somehow?"

I felt like an idiot asking this, but I had to know what was going on. He looked troubled and took a few minutes before he answered me.

"Janice, evil is a very real thing in this world and in the spirit world."

"Do you mean the devil?" I asked.

"He'll try all kinds of tricks to distract us from the mission God has imparted on us. The more you pray, the harder he'll try to stop you. The worst thing you can do is give in or allow doubt to cloud your mind. Remember, the Lord never asks more of us than we can handle."

I was truly stunned, first, that he believed in the devil and second, that the devil might be after me.

"How is your grandmother? We've missed having her here since she's been ill."

Ill? What did he mean ill? "Oh, she's fine," I said.

"Well, please give her our regards. The prayer group has been working double time on her behalf."

"I sure will. I'd best be going. Thank you for everything, Father."

When we shook hands, he covered my stone cold, clammy hand with his warm, soft hands.

"If you have any more questions, please don't ever hesitate to ask, Janice. Pray and take care."

Gram was being a sly old fox. It was time for us to have a come-to-Jesus meeting of our own. I called. She didn't answer the phone. It would have to wait until the morning.

❖

I took Father B.'s advice and I started praying up a storm. That night, the pictures faded away and I slept a dreamless sleep. In the morning, I had a new problem. When I woke up, I found my entire bed covered in white feathers. I sat bolt upright. Only the space where my body lay was free of plumage. It was like a fluffy chalk outline. I searched around, thinking an enormous bird had gotten in somehow and Rags had murdered it. There was no evidence of any bird. I found Rags upside down in a sunbeam, passed out on the carpet. There was not a bother on him. I called Annie in a panic.

"What color are they?" she asked.

It was odd that this was her first question.

"White."

"Did you check your pillows for holes?"

"I have foam pillows," I said. "I can't afford the feathery kind."

"They're probably from your spirit guides or spirit angels. I wouldn't worry about it. It's a good sign. It's certainly nothing to cause alarm. More importantly, how is your pregnancy coming along?"

How was this not alarming? I'd woken up surrounded in feathers like a plucked chicken.

"Fine."

I'd skipped a few appointments. Dr. Williams was on me about my lack of weight gain. I was holding off on seeing him until I'd put on a few pounds. He was also nagging me about things that were none of his business. He wanted to know how I'd planned to pay for things that the baby needed and if I'd started childbirth classes yet. He asked who my delivery coach was.

I said that unlike some of his other patients, being pregnant wasn't all I had going on. In the waiting room, I saw the other women in their designer maternity clothes. I knew they were judging me. I also knew I'd eventually get around to dealing with all the details, but I didn't know when.

Right then, I wanted to ask Annie to be my delivery coach. She had such a natural way of bringing me down off ledges. I'd considered asking Stefania, but I knew Claire would turn it into a problem. Gram would only make me nervous. Cilla might be upset if I picked someone else, but I was still furious with her. I decided it could wait a bit longer. I'd been handling things alone just fine. Besides it was the kind of question you should ask in person. Instead, I filled Annie in on my meeting with Father B.

"I agree. I think prayer is an excellent idea. Did you get the protective gemstones that I mentioned? Have you been doing the clearing exercises and asking for protection?"

"I keep forgetting."

"It's important, Janice. If you're going to open yourself up to this, you need to learn how to protect yourself as well. Tuning out is necessary sometimes so that it doesn't become exhausting."

"Right. Well, how do I tune out?" It wasn't as easy as changing a radio station.

"I have some special prayer-like incantations. I'll e-mail them to you. Some people say alcohol helps. Of course, I would not recommend that in your case. It's only a temporary fix with addictive consequences. Management is always best."

"Thanks, Annie."

❖

My jewelry problem was getting worse. Ever since Gram had given me her Irish Claddagh ring on my sixteenth birthday, I'd never taken it off. It had started to irritate my finger. While I vacuumed the feathers, I slipped the ring off and found the band had nearly split in two. My mornings were still temporarily free. Mel hadn't gotten around to rearranging the schedule. After breakfast, I went to the jewelry store.

"Let's have a look," the jeweler said, studying the ring while I studied him. It wasn't every day you saw a man with a ponytail. He struck me as someone who hung out in the same sorts of places as Brian and Alex. When he spoke, he put one hand on his hip and used his other hand like a prop. He held the ring in two fingers, sticking his pinky out. "Hmm. This is highly unusual."

"I know." He didn't know the half of it. What was I going to say? That I thought the devil was out to get me.

"Do you work with chemicals?" He asked.

"No. I work with patients. I do clean their rooms, but I always wear gloves."

"Well, sometimes cleaning agents can weaken precious metals. I would suggest removing your rings when you work, shower, or do any cleaning."

"OK."

"I can have it back to you a few days."

"That's great," I said. "Thanks."

While he wrote up the slip, I looked through the jewelry cases. He sold decorative gemstones. "Do you happen to have any quartz?" I asked.

"As a matter of fact, I do," he said, sifting through the case until he found what he was looking for. He dropped a small clear stone into my palm. It didn't look like a protective force against negative energy. It looked like a pebble I might find on the beach.

"We sell all of these assorted stones," he said, pulling out a tray of colorful rocks. "If you buy three or more, I'll throw in a free velvet satchel to keep them in. Let me know if I can be of any further assistance."

I culled through the stones until I found a lapis lazuli for clarity and an amethyst for spiritual wisdom. "I'll take these two," I said, laying the stones on the counter.

"Those are excellent choices. With tax, the total comes to six dollars and thirty cents. Here is your slip for the ring. You can pay for the repairs when you come back. I also sell gemstone jewelry, if you're ever interested."

"Thanks," I said. "I'll keep that in mind."

First, I had to get my current jewelry protection problem solved. I hoped the little gems would do the trick, but I wasn't at all positive it would be enough. As for my own personal protection, I said another prayer. While I prayed, I imagined a miniature devil lazing on my shoulder with a tiny pitchfork and zapping me every chance he got. It was my job to see that his efforts weren't successful, the nasty little bastard.

CHAPTER EIGHTEEN
Scrutiny

For I know nothing by myself; yet am I not hereby justified: but he that judgeth me is the Lord. —Corinthians 4:4, KJV

Hassan brings me dinner and asks, "So, what else did you see?" He'd left me with the pictures, hoping that they'd draw more thoughts out of me.

"I saw a rock band," I answered. "There were crowds of people running and screaming. I sensed water nearby but at the same time, I saw tall buildings close together, like in a city."

"That's very good, Janice. Still, I think we'll keep the blindfold on you for a little while longer."

This was what I got for trusting a terrorist.

"Open," he says, sliding a spoonful of food into my mouth. "Since you've been accommodating, I'll share something with you. Do you want to know how easily I fooled your friend?"

Which friend does he mean? What has he done now? He has my attention. He acts like it's a question, but I know better than to answer. Anyway, my mouth is full. He clearly isn't interested in my thoughts. Hassan's smug attitude makes me want to reach for my hidden fork and stab him with it. While he spouts off, I imagine blood pouring from his neck and flowing like the classical music.

"Americans. You're so trusting and open. You tell the whole world your business on social media sites, even though no one really cares. You have no shame."

He's right. Half of the time, I don't even remember what I have or haven't said online. It's the worst when I go online after having a drink or two. I'm trying to think of what I might have said that led to them capturing me. I can't think of anything.

"And your media, they're such a bunch of whores," he says. "With very little effort I found a reporter who couldn't wait to lead me to someone who led to your friend with the CIA, Ken Parkerson. He's not such a clever boy. They usually train them better. The agency must be slipping. I thought about taking Mr. Parkerson, before I found out about you."

Every blessed time I don't listen to my gut, I end up being sorry.

"Mr. Parkerson led to Pricilla, your portly friend and an easy target for information."

Cilla's life lacks excitement, so she meddles in other people's lives. My day to day is so full of naturally occurring drama I never need to go looking for any more. Hassan was pleased with himself. I chewed and fantasizing about stabbing my fork into his meatballs. This would have been a better form of justice.

"I sent Pricilla a friend request with a phony profile," he said. "I called myself Mike Jacobson and I posted some pictures of an American model."

"Open," he says pressing the fork to my lips. My hands move to the mattress, gripping the edge of the bed. My right hand is so close I could reach for my secret fork.

"I told Pricilla we had been classmates together in college. If she had checked, she might have figured out that it was all a lie. Over the course of a few weeks, I continued to compliment her. I asked her if she had a boyfriend. Before long, I knew everything about her and about you."

Cilla was to blame. I should've known. I let my hand drop and opened my mouth while he went on talking.

"With a few leading questions, I learned that you were involved in this big story on the news. It was funny. I had started out planning to kill your CIA friend. That would have been a big coup, but much too high profile. I might need to finish that job, if you fail at yours."

Can I blame Cilla or does the blame rest on my own shoulders, for not keeping my big mouth shut?

"I thought," he said, "that you would break more readily and your disappearance was easier to explain. It's been such a bonus to discover your hidden talents. Once we had acquired our information, we originally planned to kill you and dump your body somewhere. Because of your mother's reputation, everyone would assume you had run off. They would soon forget all about little Janice Morrison."

The curse of Dee strikes again. Will I ever escape it? Hassan's last comment stung. Had they all forgotten about me already? Did they think I had run away? Did they think I could leave Jessie the way Dee left me? I can't die and have her growing up thinking that.

"It's terrible when your own friends betray you. I know. I've been there myself," he said.

"Why do you kill people?" I asked. "That's not part of God's plan, no matter what you think."

"And you would know God's plan? You are a good guesser. You are maybe even a better manipulator. However, you are still a liar and an infidel."

❖

Before Jessie was born, Claire had tried to make my life hell. She confused me with legal documents and convinced me she was acting within the boundaries of the law. Claire didn't count on my knowing any lawyers, especially two as competent as Brian and Alex. The stress nearly sent me into premature labor, but she managed to get her way. For all I know, she might still be up to her old tricks, trying to convince everyone I'd abandoned Jessie. The lord surely works in mysterious ways.

❖

I missed Mass for two weeks straight. I hadn't seen Gram and I could only blame myself for being ignorant of her illness, that and Catholic guilt.

When Gram and I finally reconciled, we were both upset by Father B.'s homily about forgiveness. He went on about how secrets can eat a person up inside just like a cancer and the only way to purge your soul was to ferret the secrets out. The body and the soul needed cleansing or else they would start to deteriorate. My soul was surely a bit rank.

At breakfast, Gram was studying me. In retrospect, she knew me inside out and had to suspect something. Mine wasn't the first surprise pregnancy she had endured. It was more of a family tradition.

Dr. Williams was worried. At nearly five months pregnant, I still had only put on nine pounds. I hid my weight easily under a big sweatshirt, but I felt pudgy and my appetite was giving me away. Normally, I never ate more than a scrawny bird. After Mass at our usual breakfast haunt, I was putting food away like a squirrel saving for winter. Up to my elbows in the house special, I gobbled eggs, sausages, pancakes, and home fries smothered in catsup. Just thinking about it, I want to eat it all again. According to Dr. Williams, the problem was that I was underweight to begin with and should have gained more not less than the average woman who was with child.

I started to cave under Gram's scrutiny. Only every time I opened my mouth to tell her I was pregnant, I shoveled more food into it instead. I dodged the bullet by asking Gram about auxiliary prayer. Throughout breakfast, she went on about it. I think she was pleased I'd finally taken an interest in religion. Father B. was right. She knew everything there was to know about prayer.

I wanted to ask her about the cancer I suspected she was hiding. When we were back at her cottage, I couldn't take it anymore. How could she hide this from me? I backed into it by mentioning that I'd seen Father Ballentine and he had sent his regards. "He asked how you were feeling. So, how are you feeling, Gram?"

She looked at me with a stone-faced expression. "I'm feeling as well as could be expected under the circumstances."

"Why didn't you tell me?" I asked.

"Well, Janice, I could ask you the same thing, couldn't I?"

She had me there and I couldn't deny it.

❖

Gram was tired and she went to lie down. With a guilty conscience, I started cleaning her place. I'd never seen the house in such a heinous state. As I scrubbed and rinsed, I felt like I was cleansing my soul.

After her nap, Gram went into her prayer room while I made lunch. When she came out, she said, "Janice, I believe everything will be fine." Then she hugged me. I can count on one hand the number of times this ever happened. I felt good about the whole thing afterward. If she believed it, I believed it.

Then, just as normal as can be, we drank tea, ate sandwiches and had a civilized conversation about my plans regarding the baby.

"I'm looking at different day-care options, and I plan to keep working at Safe Harbor," I said.

What I didn't say was that paying for day care would wipe out three quarters of my salary. I didn't admit I hadn't the foggiest idea about how I'd manage to stay off welfare or keep from peddling my sorry ass on the street.

"I have enough money set aside," I said, meaning the money that was supposed to be for school. Having a baby meant putting off college again, but I wasn't giving up entirely. She didn't ask how it had happened or who the father was and I didn't volunteer the information.

"So, how bad is the cancer?" I asked.

"Janice, I won't burden you with my illness," she said. "I'm handling it. People fight cancer every day. It's manageable."

That was that. If Gram didn't want to talk about something, you wouldn't get anywhere with her. My plan was to spend as much time with her as possible. I prayed for a speedy remission. The pair of us had reached a stalemate, both pretending everything was fine, when the reality was anything but. Then just when things had hit an all time low, we had a surprise visitor.

At first, I assumed it was one of Gram's friends. Through the screen door, the shape coming up the walkway looked fuzzy. As she approached the house, I didn't even realize it was Claire. She tapped the wood on the outer storm door. I could see her fighting the urge to peer in. I went over and pushed the door open. A sense of alarm obvious on her face, her eyes moved directly to my belly and she fixated on it.

"Claire," I said. "What a surprise. What brings you down here?"

I left out the word *pleasant* because it wasn't. I didn't think Claire missed this little detail. Since Gram and Claire had never met, Gram mistook the visit for a friendly one.

"Janice, invite your friend in. Don't leave her standing on the porch. I'll get another cup of tea."

Against my better judgment, I moved aside to let Claire in. I saw her looking around the room, and was glad I'd cleaned up. I'm sure the house still looked like a hovel to her. Gram set the tea down on the table and extended her hand.

"Beatrice Morrison," Gram said. "Won't you have a seat, miss?"

Claire inspected the chair, clearly worried she might get something sticky on her spiffy outfit. Not wanting to appear rude, she slid her skinny butt into the seat.

"O'Neil," she said. "Claire O'Neil."

"So, Mrs. O'Neil, are you Janice's supervisor at Safe Harbor?" Gram asked.

Claire shuddered at the idea of being mistaken for Mel.

"No," she snapped. "I am not. Janice has never mentioned me?" She shot me a dirty look. The room fell uncomfortably silent. Claire seemed shocked Gram had no idea who she was.

"No, I'm afraid not. How do you two know each other?" Gram asked.

Claire was at a loss for words, unprepared to discuss our relationship. Having to put it into words made the whole situation feel a little too intimate. Who was she to me? She was not my mother-in-law, but she was the grandmother of my unborn child. Claire looked at me and then at Gram. She didn't seem to know what to say.

"Janice, perhaps this would be easier if you explained to your grandmother why I'm here." They both looked at me expectantly.

I was enjoying watching Claire squirm too much to make life easier on her. "Why are you here, Claire?" I asked.

"I am here because I want to make sure that there won't be any trouble when the baby arrives," she said.

Gram was finally on board the sinking ship with the rest of us. Her expression changed from polite to confused tolerance.

"What do you mean by that, miss?" Gram asked. "What was the name again?"

"O'Neil. Mrs. O'Neil. My son, Jason, is an unfortunate victim in this whole mess."

I had to hold back my own hand. It occurred to me then that I'd never be truly free of this woman or her devious son. It would have felt good to knock her out of her chair, but then what would I do. I'd be having my baby behind bars.

"Is there a Mr. Morrison?" Claire asked. "Perhaps he should join us?"

"No. I'm afraid he's no longer with us," Gram said. She gave the impression Grandpa had died as opposed to having run off with a floozy. I raised one eyebrow but I let it go. Good on you, Gram, I thought.

"Sunday is a sacred day in our household, Mrs. O'Neil. We would appreciate you stating your business and then being on your way."

Years earlier, I'd seen Gram like this. At the rectory, I had been helping unpack the new hymnal books. Gram had a meeting with a man who represented what she called an unsavory charitable organization. He'd tried to extort money from the church. When Gram caught wind of this, the man wished he had never set foot in our little parish. Sitting at the kitchen table with Claire, Gram had the same look in her eye.

"Well," Claire said. "I'm sure we can both agree that what happened was an unfortunate *accident*. Our family is moving forward and we are hoping yours will do the same. It's just a shame we weren't all privy to the pregnancy sooner. We might have been able to seek alternative measures."

Claire seemed to be under the mistaken impression that she and Gram were paddling on the same side of the canoe. Gram stiffened and sat bolt upright. "What do mean by *alternative*?"

I was sick of looking at Claire. She had a lot of nerve showing up on our doorstep uninvited. I wanted her gone, so I decided to cut her crap with a blunt knife. "Gram, Claire thinks I should've had an abortion and now she's worried I purposely slept with her son because I'm after her money. Does that about cover it, Claire?"

My comments had the desired effect. Gram was up and out of her chair. "Mrs. O'Neil, please leave my home! You're not welcome here."

Claire anchored herself in her chair. "Mrs. Morrison, I understand you're upset, we both are, but taking this out on me is a grave mistake. She's the one you should be angry at," she said, wagging her bony finger at me. Then she pulled a white envelope out of her purse. "I want you to know that I have one of the best lawyers in the state. I asked him to put this together for you. It's the only offer we plan to make."

She laid the envelope on the table, waved her manicured hand in my direction and talked about me as if I were invisible. "It's more than reasonable. Under the circumstances, it's considerably more than she deserves. There is an agreement she'll need to sign to state that she will not have any further contact with Jason or any member of our family. Most importantly, the baby absolutely *cannot* take our name. Please have it back to me by the week's end. I'd like to put this whole nasty business behind me."

It took all of my reserve not to pop her one in her little pinched nose. Gram's lips had vanished into a straight thin line and her eyes glowed like charcoal stoked with kerosene. Gram picked up the envelope and opened the back door.

"Mrs. O'Neil, I want you to know that the sheriff is a close personal friend of mine. If you don't get out of my house immediately, I'll have you arrested for trespassing and harassment."

They both stood face to face. Neither of them gave an inch.

"And take this with you," Gram whipped the envelope at Claire, hitting her square in the face and added, "you self-important bitch."

Claire staggered backward in her skinny heels, nearly falling out the door. I couldn't help but laugh. She grimaced as she recovered.

"Have it your way," Claire hissed, snatching the envelope off the floor and walking out the door. Just beyond the threshold, she stopped on the stairs and turned around. "I never did understand people like you. You have more pride than sense."

The screen door snapped shut behind her. The door to the chapel room then slammed. It still makes me laugh to think about the look on Claire's face, with her nostrils flaring and her beady eyes glowering. She left the cottage with smoke on her heels and steam coming out of her ears. All the while, her tidy black bob never budged an inch.

I sat alone at the kitchen table, drinking my stone-cold tea and watching the sun slip into the Chesapeake Bay, a big pregnant ball of fire. Once again, I had created one hell of a shit storm.

CHAPTER NINETEEN
Foreshadowing

Have we not all one father? Hath not one God created us? Why do we deal treacherously every man against his brother, by profaning the covenant of our fathers? —Malachi 2:10, KJV

I have a confession to make, one I should've made earlier, I became so angry over Gram's illness, I'd told the voices to stop communicating altogether and they did. It was a relief in the beginning, but then I started to miss them a little. It was lonely to be with my own thoughts again after I'd grown accustomed to having so much company.

As I shunned the voices, they were slow to return to me. I kept praying, asking, and begging, but was met only by echoing silence and my own empty thoughts. I rejected my image staring back at me through the psychic mirror.

I finally understood the puzzle I needed to solve and the reality of my circumstances. I had to rely on myself. I was all that I had left.

Six months pregnant, I so badly wanted to go out and start looking at baby things, but I was stuck with the Internet and only had enough money for window-shopping anyway. How would I ever afford motherhood?

Ken had sent a message. Despite the fact that I had already considered doing what he was asking me to do, I hate it when people meddle in my business.

Janice,

I've known you for a long time, and I know you are a forgiving person. Will you please consider forgiving Pricilla? Call me if you need anything. I hope you know I'm always here for you.

Best, Ken

❖

I had ignored all of Cilla's urgent messages, and this happened as a result. Cilla's idea of urgency probably involved running out of milk or having a pimple that wouldn't go away. She knew nothing of real problems. I was still annoyed with her. Since our falling out, I'd been making sure that my work relationships were strictly professional. I didn't even tell her the story about Claire, even though I was dying to tell her. I called Stefania instead.

OK. Maybe I was being too hard. I might have been a little jealous of Cilla's boring normalcy. When your life is a mess, though, it's tough to deal with someone who doesn't have any real problems. After I ignored Ken's message, I got another one from Cilla.

❖

Janice,

Please don't stay mad! I slipped and told Ken about the baby and the tunnel thing. I swear I didn't get into all of your premonitions. I'm sorry! I thought he should know about the potential danger. I should have asked you first. I know that I was wrong. I've been a bad friend and I don't deserve your friendship, but I hope you'll forgive me anyway.

YBF (Still, I hope!) Cilla

❖

Why was I obligated to forgiveness? She hadn't lasted a minute at keeping her big mouth shut. I'd kept plenty of things private for her, but she couldn't do the same. When the people you depend on most let you down, the lack of trust becomes a permanent wedge between you. It can splinter and irritate over time, but it never really goes away.

I didn't send a message back to either of them. The only reason I'd even considered easing up on my anger was that being angry all the time was exhausting. Still, they would both have to work to earn my trust back.

I missed having my talks with Stefania, and I was sick of everyone and everything else in my life. As I dialed her number, my mind wandered back to Christmas night, before the tide of my life turned to raw sewage.

"Stefania, how's life?"

"Janeeze, how nice to hear your voice."

"How are things with the O'Neil's?"

"No good."

"Stefania? What's wrong? You're still working there, aren't you?"

"Oh, yes, but this week I wish I wasn't. Listen, Janeeze, I wanted to call you. Nanny's not well. They think that maybe she has a week or so left to live."

"Oh."

"Janeeze?"

"I've got to go," I said.

"I'm sorry. I'll let you know when Nanny passes away. Let's have coffee next week. We'll talk."

"OK." I knew it was coming, but I had put it out of my mind.

❖

The next day at work, Cilla kept apologizing and trying to get me to laugh. When I have a bug up my butt, it's best to steer clear of me. I'm a mule that way. By the end of the day, Cilla had worn me down with her talk of a baby shower. I explained to Cilla that I would have eventually told Ken I was pregnant and I didn't even care about him knowing about the other stuff. What bothered me was the lack of control that I had over my own secrets. They were my secrets. I wanted someone in my life I could count on. Was I asking too much?

Maybe it was all foreshadowing of how things would only get worse from there on out.

Looking perturbed, Mel caught me in the kitchen as I was scraping some trays. "Janice, you have a visitor. Make it snappy. Mrs. James needs fresh linens."

"I'm not expecting anybody." I checked my watch. It was stuck at 9:00 a.m.

"That's an odd choice of words, Janice. She's at the front desk."

I hoped it was Stefania or Gram. Either of them would've been a nice surprise. I wasn't so lucky.

"Well, just look at you, like mother like daughter, I guess." Dee said opening her arms and inviting me into a hug. I crossed my arms over my chest, resting them on my baby bump.

"What in the hell do you want?" I asked.

From the front desk, the wide-eyed receptionist looked from me to Dee and back again. Then she shuffled off toward Mel's office with paperwork in her hands. I noticed she didn't shut the office door.

"I came to see my baby, who is having a baby. Oh my goodness, I can't believe this." She reached over and patted my belly. "I'm way too young to be a grandmother."

Stiffening, I took a giant step backward. She had a hell of a lot of nerve. "Ha! It's all about you now isn't always? Well, I'm thinking your mirror must have broken. Life on the road has not been kind."

She sucked in her gut and attempted to smooth her frizzy mop with both of her hands. In truth, she looked better than I had expected. Except for the fact that she was thirty-eight years old and I was pregnant, she could have been my twin sister.

"Janice, baby, I'm not here to fight with you."

"Why are you here?"

"Because mamma needs me and you're having a baby."

"Lie, lie, lie or is it still just an easy lay? The same old Dee. I know you planned on coming here before you found out about the baby. So, how much will it take to get you on the next bus out of town? One hundred? Two hundred?"

"You can't pay me off to stay out of your life. I'm still your mother, whether you like it or not."

"No. I don't have a mother. I only have a grandmother. It's been that way for fifteen years. I have to get back to work. I'm sure you can figure out how to leave."

❖

Something made me hesitate with the fork again. Dammit! Again, I didn't risk it when it was just Hassan and me. Even now, I can't commit murder. It's harder than you might think to become a killer. Something inside would have to snap in two. That's not why I have this gift.

I pick at the grout like a sculptor carving life out of stone, until only a small pebble holds the square of glass in place. I can now pop it out at will. Peering outside, I smooth the toothpaste into place. The last of the leaves has fallen. The trees are stark and naked against the gray sky. The "for sale" sign next door bends under the weight of the wind. The house is still empty.

When the door handle rattles, I jump.

"Janice, unlock this door immediately!" Hassan shouts.

"I'm just getting dressed!" I yell back, flushing the toilet, hiding the fork, and fumbling with the lock. He comes in and I watch him look around suspiciously. I realize too late that I've forgotten the blindfold. He stops at the window, inspects it, and then looks at me with narrow eyes. I pull the blindfold down to hide mine.

"No more locking the door," he says.

"Sorry. It's an old habit."

In my room, I have company. No one talks to me. They only talk to each other, but I feel them standing over me and yelling into my ears. Bo, Ape, and Chief are all here. Chief hasn't been here in a while. With him here, the tension weighs heavily in the air like wet wool blanket. I have him figured for the group's leader, the one they talk to on the phone. The others seem uptight and more official because he's here.

The curiosity is killing me. I know Hassan's face, but I want to know what the rest look like. So far, I've failed to get my blindfold removed. My logic is silly, but I convince myself they wouldn't bother to blindfold me if they were going to kill me. In a way, it's an extra layer of protection.

They've stopped yelling. Bo touches the blade to my arm and then turns it to its sharp point. Ape is there as a reinforcement, as if a ninety-eight-pound terrified female requires all of this manpower. Chief and Bo dictate.

"If you lie, we'll dump your body where it will never be found. You'll be just another runaway who left her baby motherless. Do you choose life?" Hassan asks.

"Yes," I answer, wondering how many times this has happened. How many stories left untold?

"Good," he says, removing my blindfold. Circled around me I see Hassan, Saif, Ahmed, and Muhammad, aka English, Ape, Bo, and Chief. I'm blinking, forcing my eyes to adjust when Hassan asks me a question.

"In your visions, have you seen our faces among the faces of the dead?"

CHAPTER TWENTY
Psychopath

With my third trimester underway, I'd managed to weather Claire's backlash and was growing into a ripe hippopotamus. Once the world knew she was coming, Jessie refused to stay hidden any longer.

Doctor Williams finally stopped pestering me about my weight. I lied and told him I had a birth plan. I planned to give birth. That was my plan. Regardless, he started on a new mission.

"Young lady, you're too inexperienced to know better right now, but if you decide against the pain medication, I can assure you that you will be sorry. I've delivered many, many babies for girls in your condition, and I have the experience to know what's best for you."

"Well, Dr. Williams, I appreciate your concern, but like I said, you can write down no drugs in that file of yours, and I mean no drugs. I assure you, I won't be sorry."

Cilla agreed with me 100 percent on the drug thing, but I suspected she would give it some more thought whenever her time came.

"If I'm on another delivery, the doctor who is on call will go by what's listed in your file," he said.

"That's fine, Dr. Williams. No one really knows what the long-term side effects of those drugs are on babies. Only time will tell and the studies are inconclusive."

This sure shut him up. I actually heard his jaw snap shut.

"Just so you know, young lady, if you ask for medication when it's too late, they won't be able to administer it."

"Don't worry," I said. "I won't."

❖

One Saturday, I found myself with nothing left to fit over my girth. Stefania came to my apartment with a giant bag of maternity clothes she'd gathered from her relatives. There were some pretty things, but I told her, "You can put a ball gown on an elephant, but it won't make her a princess."

She handed me a container of her mom's famous eggplant Parmesan. I popped it open and started eating it. I'd never considered eating an eggplant before I met Stefania. I offered her some.

"No, thank you," she said. "I never eat between meals. I'm so glad you are eating. The baby needs to grow. Are you having enough pasta?"

"I eat enough of everything. If she's the one growing, why do I feel like Jabba the Hut?"

"I don't know this Jabba, but you look fantastico. Wait a minute." She reached over and plucked something from my hair. "That's strange." She opened her palm to find a fluffy white feather. "Look, you're shedding."

I hadn't had another feather episode quite like the big one, but now they appeared everywhere in small doses. They were in my car, on my clothes, and in my hair. I started a collection in a shoebox, along with my jewelry and the protective stones.

Over coffee, Stefania confessed to not liking my replacement, Nurse Miller. In a way, hearing this made me feel better, but things were worse for Nanny. I moved her up on my prayer list.

"This Nurse Miller, she's so lazy. She moves like a turtle and sits around reading magazines. Then she has a nerve to order me around, telling me bring up the meals. Why should I do her job? I don't work for her and I said so."

"Yeah, you're right. I know her. She gives Cilla all her nursing work, while she takes a million cigarette breaks and makes three times our salary. How do some people get away with doing nothing while the rest of us work like dogs?"

"I don't know," Stefania said, shaking her head.

"Speaking of dogs how's Francis?" I asked.

"Oh, *il povero cane*. Claire will put him out when Nanny is gone."

"You mean *down*? She can't do that. Stefania, please kidnap him. I'll take him."

"What will you do with a dog? What will Mr. Fluffy think?" She asked, looking at Rags, curled in a ball on my couch.

"I don't know. He might like some company."

"I'll find someone to take him. Claire's been a monster, but you'll like this. I put extra onions and garlic in everything. They give her the upset stomach."

"That's awesome." I laughed. "I hope she has massive gas."

"After Claire fired you, she said, 'Don't get any ideas.' Please. As if I would want anything to do with her pig of a son after what he did. I want to spit on her face. I said, 'Don't you worry. He's not good enough for me.'"

"What? Stefania, you should be careful. She'll fire you next. What did she say?"

"I'm a coward. I said it in Italian. I wish I was more like your grandmother. If only I could have been there. When I quit, I will give her an earful in English."

"Let me know. I'll come for the show." I laughed. "God, I miss hanging out with you."

"Come to my house for dinner Sunday. Everyone's been asking about you, especially Francesco," she said, raising her eyebrow.

"I'd love to." I felt my face turning bright red.

"He's my brother, Janeeze. I love him, even though he's always a pest. I have to warn you. Listen, the reason we left Naples was to keep Francesco from running with the gangs. My cousins in Naples are a bunch of thieves."

"Stefania, aren't you being too harsh."

"No. I'm serious. They rob people in their sleep."

"What? What if they get caught?"

"*Ai*. They're like ninjas. They never get caught. They think they are big men, acting like gangsters. It's crazy."

"What if someone woke up and saw them?"

"They use the sleeping gas. When the people wake up, everything is gone. Oh, Janice. My brother is so hopeless. When he goes to Naples, he's always in trouble. So you see, he is bad news."

I sloughed it off. For some reason, after hearing that story, I was even more attracted to Francesco than I'd ever been before. As much as I didn't want to know, I couldn't help but ask, "Speaking of bad news, has Jason been around?"

"No," Stefania said. "Thank goodness. He's too busy with school. Over the summer, he'll be working for one of Dick's friends in Washington DC. He starts medical school in September. At least he will stay out of trouble that way. They are having a huge graduation party with hundreds of people. I've been cooking forever and freezing things. I don't know when the party will be because of Nanny's health. She's hanging on."

I shuddered to think of Jason as a doctor. He didn't have a caring bone in his body. He'll be one of those creepy doctors—the kind who makes you uncomfortable when there is nothing between you and them but a hospital gown.

The situation with Claire firing me was a blessing of sorts. It gave me more time for doctors, Gram's doctors and mine. I put my head down and started to cry.

"Hey, forget about that *idiota*," she said, patting my back. "You'll be a great mother. Don't worry. I'll help you. You'll be fine."

"I know. I know you're right," I said.

It wasn't Jason or the baby. It was that Gram had told me she was in remission and she didn't need any more doctors' appointments. It could have been the prayers. Miracles do happen but it didn't jive with what the doctors had said before. My plan was to spend as much time with her as possible. You just never know when God would call your number.

❖

I used to think becoming psychic was the worst thing that had ever happened to me. That was before pregnancy, before Gram's cancer, before the return of dastardly Dee, and before my kidnapping. In light of the state of my life, why would I fear death? It'd be a welcome change. I could escape by dying. No one else would get hurt, except for a slew of strangers at the new target, the shopping mall.

If I admit I've seen all of their faces, will my friends and I suffer? If I say I haven't seen them, will my friends and I suffer?

Next to Hassan, Saif is enormous and hairy. His full black beard makes him look like a pirate. Ahmed, like his odor, is hideous, and skeletal. His skin pockmarked, from either burns or scars. Muhammad is older than the rest of them. He wears white from head to toe, and he has a long gray beard. If I didn't know any better, I'd say his face looked kind. I roll the dice and brace myself.

"Yes," I say, "I've seen all of you."

❖

Because the premonitions had become routine and my pregnancy was out in the open, I felt like less of a liar. It was good the voices warned me whenever one of my patients was dying so I could add them to my prayers. I even managed to learn how to turn my psychosis off and on.

In a nearly full journal, I kept making notes about each new premonition. I wrote in code, using initials. Feeling like the angel of death, my need to do something positive led to meddling.

Keeping vigil over those on the great escalator to heaven, I secretly called my patients relatives and coaxed a final visit out of them. I was careful. If Mel had found out what I'd been up to, she'd have strung me up. How would I ever explain myself? On the phone, I'd always make up something logical. I'd say, "He's been asking for you." Or "I think you'd better come. Her color looks bad." I also identified myself as Nurse Miller. In light of the call, most people don't remember the name of the caller. Even if it did come back to haunt me I'd find a way to deal with it.

Cilla was flat out with the planning of the baby shower for me, so I let go my anger. The idea of the shower lessened the burden of acquiring baby things. Cilla and Stefania were in cahoots and planned to have the party at *Basilico*. With Cilla as the head of the planning committee, there was no hope of it being a surprise. After making her swear not to ask a bunch of questions about psychic phenomena, I finally let Cilla have Annie's number. Mrs. S. and Gram were in on it as well. Unfortunately, even though I'd managed to avoid her, Dee had still not left town.

After surprises, the second thing I most despise is being the center of attention. I wasn't looking forward to the baby shower, but I desperately needed things for Jessie. I tried my hardest to cooperate.

Cilla took me to one of those giant warehouse stores full of baby products. She dragged me around to register for things she thought I would need. The clerk gave us this electronic gizmo to zap things with that linked the items to my name in the store's computer.

I wasn't sure why I had to register for so much stuff. I couldn't imagine who was going to buy all of these things or where I'd put them all if they did. I only knew a few people. Most of them were just as broke as I was and baby furniture and clothes were so darned expensive.

Back in the time of settlers, people used dresser drawers for cradles. After seeing the prices of the cribs, I thought this idea seemed smart. I figured I'd rearrange my clothes and put a soft blanket in my bottom drawer. I'd save spending three months of my salary on a crib.

To appease Cilla, I went ahead and picked one out anyway. Standing in front of the most beautiful round, white crib, I actually lost my breath for a minute. It had the most gorgeous eyelet bedding and accessories. A dream nursery for any baby if only you had all of the money in world.

I imagined after Jason became a surgeon, he'd find some perfect little wife and their babies would have a beautiful nursery with everything and then some. I bet he'll never tell his perfect future wife the truth about Jessie and me. I couldn't take my eyes off that crib.

"Oh, Janice," Cilla said. "Look at this rocking chair. You have to register for this."

I looked at the price tag first. "Cilla, this chair is three hundred dollars. I can get one at the Salvation Army for about thirty bucks and repaint it. Pity they don't have a registry at Sal's."

"Oh, Janice! You can't paint while you're pregnant."

She snatched the gizmo and zapped the price ticket. Then she zapped the crazy expensive white crib and all of the accessories. Cilla was more excited about the whole thing than I was. With my due date fast approaching, panic had set in. How was I ever going to take care of a baby when I could barely take care of myself? Dee's face flashed across my mind.

She was supposedly staying with a friend, but whenever the spirit moved her, she dropped in on Gram. As such, I was avoiding the cottage and only saw Gram at church.

As if she could read my mind, Cilla asked, "Have you seen your mom?"

"Please, don't call her that. No, I haven't seen Dee. If you want me to show up, you best not dare invite her to this shower."

"Janice, I'm sure she expects to be invited."

"I don't care what she expects. I expected a mother and instead I got a psychopath. Spare me from having to worry about her feelings."

"I'm sorry," Cilla said. "You're right. Maybe she'll leave town before then. You know, Nurse Miller said she saw Dee singing at the Snake Pit Bar."

Finally an explanation her sudden visit. She had some gig. She hadn't come for Gram or me.

"Well," I said. "That's the perfect place for her, now isn't it?"

Maybe it was the togetherness, but I found myself opening up to Cilla again. A strange new thing had begun happening at church, and I needed to bend someone's ear about it. Since I'd confided in Father B., I felt like he was preaching directly to me during Mass.

"Last week, I was up all night fretting about why God gave me this ability," I said to Cilla. "On Sunday morning, I'm sitting there with Gram. We're listening to Father B. read the scripture about how Job was a reluctant prophet. Even in the full church, I could've sworn he was looking right at me. I thought maybe he was trying to send me a message or give me answers through the scripture, but he was just reading the scripture for the day. The books are all printed way in advance, so how could that be? Right?"

"Janice, don't take this the wrong way, but is it possible you're being a little self-centered? Isn't it a sin to think so highly of yourself that you believe the whole Mass is centered entirely around you?"

I have to admit, I was truly offended. Cilla just wasn't getting what I was saying. First, she wasn't Catholic and second, I wasn't sure which religion she followed because she never mentioned any. Not that there was anything wrong with belonging with a different faith, I respect that, but Cilla didn't even attend church regularly.

Cilla was usually levelheaded about these things. It occurred to me maybe she was jealous. I was getting all of this attention with the pregnancy and the premonitions. Maybe it was just more than she could take. I let it drop.

"You know something, Cilla? You might be right. Maybe my head is swelling as much as my middle. I'm sure it's a sin to be so boastful."

I'd planned to talk to Bridge or Annie about it. They were the only ones who really got the supernatural stuff. Annie understood how every time I doubted the messages or thought it was all in my imagination, I'd get this weird impulse to look in a certain direction. Lo and behold, I'd see some undeniable symbol of the Lord. It might be a shadow in the shape of a crucifix or a statue of Mary on someone's lawn.

Bridge was the one I called when I was having nightmares that something was trying to suffocate me. In my dream, I'd yell as loud as I could at the evil thing, but my voice sounded like it was in slow motion, like a record played in reverse. When I woke up, sometimes I'd find a sheet or my shirt wrapped around my neck. Then one day, it was no longer just a nightmare, my crucifix fell off the wall. Evil signs had manifested in real life. Bridge said, "Pray, pray, pray and be careful Janice. I'm worried you're in over your head."

❖

There's a problem with sharing any burden. No matter how much you want to believe people when they say, they won't tell a living soul, it's usually the first thing they do. It's hard not slip and confide in someone when you spend most of your time with them. So I blame myself above all others.

Our shared history told me better than to tell Cilla anything that I didn't want broadcast. She and Ken had been getting serious, and Cilla couldn't help herself from telling Ken everything that I'd told her.

Whenever I chatted with Ken online, he was short with his answers. He kept asking how I was feeling. At first, I thought he was just concerned about the baby. Then he wrote, "If I you need to talk about anything, I'm here for you." It set off the light bulb in my brain. I signed off, called Cilla, and gave her an earful.

"All right," I said. "What did you tell him this time?"

"I'm just concerned about your mental health," said Cilla. "*We* think you might need to get a professional opinion."

"Cilla, if I wanted Ken to know about all of this, I'd have told him myself. Why are you such a busybody? You know something? You're physically unable to keep a secret."

I could tell my comment stung, and I was glad.

"I'm sorry, Janice. I was only…" I could hear she was about to start bawling. This teed me off even more. She was in the wrong, yet I had to apologize again.

"You were only talking about me behind my back," I said.

"I was only trying to help. With the stress of the baby and everything, I wondered if it was all making you a little too…"

"I'm not crazy, Cilla," I said. "Something is happening to me—something beyond my control and just because you and Ken can't make it all add up like some math equation, doesn't mean it's not real!"

She didn't say anything, but I was sure I could hear her sniffling.

"I have to get some sleep," I said. "Do me a favor, OK? Don't go getting anyone else's opinion on my mental state. I'm happy to go crazy all by myself. Thank you very much."

I hung up feeling angrier than I'd started out. Ken tried to chat with me again a few minutes later, no doubt after a frantic call from Cilla. I ignored him, turned off the computer, and turned on the TV.

The news was on. A newscaster said, "US forces leveled an Al Qaeda stronghold using drones. Ayman Al Hasara, a top Al Qaeda leader, is thought to be among those killed, along with several civilian casualties."

In truth, it struck a nerve. I had begun to question my own sanity. After all I'd been through, if I allowed doubt to shatter my faith, what would remain? God had chosen me for this purpose and I couldn't fail him. There was too much at stake. I had to stop talking about it. Job didn't go crying to his friends whenever God called him to task. What in the hell was my problem?

CHAPTER TWENTY-ONE
Martyrdom

Let the sighing of the prisoner come before thee; according to the greatness of thy power preserve thou those that are appointed to die. —Psalm 79:11, KJV

Why is Muhammad here? Does this mean they are ready to attack? Hassan makes a low noise. It begins like a growl and rises to a shout. They all join in, smiling and chanting.

"*Allahu akbar! Allahu akbar!*"

They chant together as they leave the room, all but one. I'm alone again with Hassan. "This sacrifice is the ultimate commitment. To die as a martyr is the greatest blessing."

I don't believe he's a killer. It's another lie. If my other instincts are right, maybe I am also right about him not hurting me.

"Why are you doing this? You're not like them. You aren't a killer."

"Janice, don't waste your witchcraft on me. With the proper motivation, anyone can be a killer. I will prove this to you."

"No. Not me. I could never murder anyone."

"You didn't want to hurt me when I slaughtered your little kitty? What about when I put your friend in the nursing home? Didn't you think that you would find justice in causing me pain?"

This is about revenge. Ask him how Hasheem died. While this thought passes through my brain, I see an explosion and a body.

"You call them your brothers, but your real brother died. That's why you joined them. Still, you're not a murder."

"You make easy assumptions. Any carnival psychic could make those leaps."

"If you don't believe in me, why haven't you killed me already?"

He looks away. He won't answer me.

"You want revenge, but you should forget your anger and go home. That's what Hasheem wants for you."

I watch the darkness settle over him like a smoky shroud. His face turns hard and he ages before my eyes.

"Janice, I am warning you. Don't you talk about my brother. You are a fool and your voices are the thoughts of a mad woman. Hasheem would never quit and he would never ask me to give up."

"He would," I say. "He can see everything now. He's on the other side, trying to protect you. It's not too late. You haven't hurt anyone yet. You could just leave. They'd never find you."

"I will leave the only one way anyone ever leaves the brotherhood, and so will you."

❖

As quickly as she had blown into town, the tornado, aka Dee, was gone again. She had left a lot of wreckage in her wake. Gram was missing some of her pain meds, some blank checks, and the money that she had hidden around the house. Luckily, I was able to alert the bank before Dee had the chance to cash any of the checks. I was just glad she had left before the baby shower.

I had missed going to Mass more than a few times with Gram. I didn't know then how I'd end up making up for that. As my belly grew, I became more and more self-conscious and made excuses for not attending. It might have been my imagination, but it felt like everyone stared at me and judged. Then again, it was probably just my guilty conscience.

Ten days before the shower, I was in an unshakeable funk. Each time I entered a patient's room I expected the worst. Everyone was holding steady, though. I walked out to the front desk, surprised to find Nurse Miller sorting through patient charts. She looked up and said, "You look like you could drop that kid at any minute."

"Shouldn't you be at the O'Neil house?" I asked.

"No more patient, no more job," she said, walking away with her arms full of charts. She left me standing there in the middle of the hall.

"Come with me," Hassan said. "I have something to show you."

I'd never been anywhere else in the house besides the closet and the bathroom. I followed Hassan down the hall. We walked through a door and went out to the garage. A large moving van sat parked in the bay. It looked just like the one that I had seen in my vision, except this one was in color, rather than black and white. He took me around to the back and pulled up the metal door. He and his partners had filled the truck to the top with bags.

"What's in them?" I asked.

"They're full of ammonium nitrate."

"What's that?"

"Fertilizer," he said.

"Hassan, are you planning on growing something?"

"You're a very funny girl, Janice. Try just the opposite."

"Nanny's funeral will be a small and private affair," Claire had told Stefania. The truth was that Claire expected hundreds to attend.

For days, Stefania cooked furiously just as she had done for Jason's graduation party weeks earlier. The rest of the Fortini family arrived the day of as reinforcements. Ciro, Enzo, Maximus, and Francesco served and tended the bar and Mrs. Fortini was on hand to assist with the cooking and preparations.

I felt badly they had my baby shower coming up on the heels of this event, but Stefania swore to me that it was her pleasure. In fact, the added event cooking and planning had led to her new business, the catering arm of *Basilico*.

For obvious reasons, I wasn't able to go to the post funeral meal. I did attend the funeral though disguised, as a member of Stefania's family, complete with a black veil I slipped into the Mass and paid my respects to Nanny. I looked like another one of Stefania's aunts who was in perpetual mourning. Claire never spotted me in the back of the church, but Jason somehow did. Getting into the car to leave, I felt someone touch my shoulder. When I turned, a shudder went through my entire body.

"Well, I didn't expect to see you here," he said.

"That makes two of us, Jason."

"You even look good pregnant," he said, looking me up and down. "Maybe we could get together some time."

His comment was so grossly inappropriate I ignored it. "I'm so sorry about your grandmother."

"Yeah. Well, she was old. It happens," he shrugged.

"I have to go, Jason."

"See you around, Janice."

Only if I don't see you coming first.

❖

A few days later, Gram called. "Janice, there's a FedEx envelope here at the house with your name on it. I didn't open it."

"I'm not expecting anything. You can go ahead and open it. Save me the stress," I said. I heard the sound of cardboard tearing.

"It's a letter from a lawyer's office. I think you'd better come over," she said.

❖

With a start, I wake from a sound sleep. The light is on. Hassan stands over me, holding something metal and shiny in his hands.

"Janice. Janice. Janice. I gave you my trust. How do you think it makes me feel to learn you've betrayed me?"

I don't say anything. I'm still bleary-eyed and trying to focus on what he's holding. "What did I do?"

"One, two, three, four, five, six, seven," he says, counting forks. "This is a set of eight, Janice. Where is number eight?"

"I don't know. How would I know? Did you ask Saif?"

"No. I'm not asking Saif. I'm asking you."

"I've only just starting eating without help. You know that. Have any forks been missing when my plate comes back? No. Because it wasn't me."

He considers this and I add, "All I'm saying is that Saif might have thrown one away by accident. It used to happen all the time at Safe Harbor."

"Your explanation seems unlikely. You came up with your answer too quickly. Speaking of harbors, I heard on the news today about a terrible boating accident in Deale, Maryland. A young couple and their friends are missing. Isn't that where your friend Annie lives? It's quite tragic."

He's lying. I know he's lying. I search my mind, but no image of Annie comes. I ask him, "Haven't I done everything you've asked me to do? Haven't I?"

"Not yet," Hassan says. "But you will."

According to the letter, Nanny had created a trust fund for my baby in the sum of one hundred thousand dollars. I started to hyperventilate. Gram handed me a paper bag and said, "Janice, I'm calling the paramedics."

"No. I'm OK," I said. "I'm OK. I just need to breathe."

My new rotund state made it hard to breathe as it was. I'd packed on an extra ten pounds during my last trimester. Suddenly I was wearing a fat suit that I hadn't adjusted to yet.

Claire had to want me dead. There was no way she'd let this set. Money wasn't everything, but it sure gave a girl a fighting chance. If I were able to keep the money, Jessie could finally break the curse of the Morrison women. The next move was up to Claire.

Bloated, uncomfortable and as graceful as a whale on dry land, I knew carrying Jessie on the inside was a heck of a lot easier than it'd be to juggle life with her on the outside. Still, I wanted my body back.

August was miserable in Maryland, with no break from the humidity. The hot, murky bay offered no escape. In my apartment, I had the world's smallest air conditioner stuffed in my window. Pouring with sweat, I parked my expanding behind in a chair right in front of the unit.

Rags pawed at the door. He wanted out and I didn't blame him. I couldn't imagine wearing a fur coat in the summer. I took him over to Mrs. S. With two air conditioning units running full force, her place was a refrigerator. She answered the door in a sweater, and let a blast of cool air escape.

"Janice, you must be so excited. It won't be long now before we get to meet this beautiful baby."

"I'm too hot to be excited. Can you take Rags for a spell? I'm worried about him and the new baby. They say cats get jealous."

"Of course, dear. You let me know when you want him back. Come in and have some tea."

Hot tea? I wanted to dunk my head in a bucket of ice tea. "Thanks, but I've got to get to work."

Two cold showers later and still sweating, I gave up. I tugged on my extra large scrubs. The fabric stuck to my skin. Within seconds, a sweat line had formed across my belly. It was a relief when I finally walked into Safe Harbor and central air conditioning.

❖

The next night, I was a guest at the Fortini home for dinner. It was a nice break from the heat, my baby woes, and the cancerous thoughts of my daily life. Now that I was an honorary part of the family, they invited me to all of their special events. That night Francesco was turning twenty-three years old.

Even on his birthday, Stefania fought with him. I'd been working on my Italian for nearly a year, so I could decipher most of their bickering. I was sitting between the pair of them and heard it all in stereo. Mama Mia. I hoped Stefania would never get angry with me.

"Stupido! Tu sei un barbone."

"Aw, Stefie. I poveri Zitella."

Francesco knew how to push Stefania's buttons in front of the family. He chose a touchy subject and called her a poor Spinster. This was somehow worse than being a bum at Francesco's age. When they fell to acting like little children, Mrs. Fortini broke up the argument, saying *"Basta così! Mangia!"*

Embarrassed by their behavior, Mrs. Fortini changed the subject to my upcoming baby shower. It seemed everyone was excited about the party and the whole family planned to attend.

"Wait," Stefania said. "The baby shower is only for the women, no men allowed."

This started a new argument.

"If it's happening in my restaurant," Mr. Fortini said, "no one can stop me from coming to the party."

"That's right, I'll be there too," Francesco added.

"You can be the waiter, that's all," Stefania said to him.

I couldn't help but smile.

Under the table, a warm hand rested on my leg just above my knee. I reached down and put my hand over Francesco's hand. This event for little Jessica Morrison would be one hell of a *festa*.

I knew Cilla would have had a fit when she found out men were going to be crashing the party. I kept this little detail to myself, knowing she could only handle so much. The shower was stressing her out even though it sounded to me as if Stefania and Mrs. Fortini were doing all of the work.

I was excited about the prospect of new baby things, but just in case, I had cleared out my dresser drawer to be ready for my new bundle. There was no one on the invitations list who would spring for the deluxe new crib.

Two days before the big day, another official document found its way to my grandmother's house with my name on it. This time, it was from Claire's fancy lawyer. I assumed it was something to counter the last letter, making that one null and void. Instead, it was a notification about a lawsuit. Claire had declared me an unfit mother and was suing for full custody of my unborn child. I dialed Brian's number in a panic.

❖

"Our cover is a rock and roll band. We take it very seriously. All of us actually play instruments," Hassan says.

I knew Hassan played the keyboards and I'd heard Saif practicing the drums. I assumed the others must have been guitarists.

"You will pose as a singer. Can you sing?"

I shrug my shoulders.

"Here are the lyrics to some songs. Start practicing."

"What is the purpose of the band?" I asked. "I don't get it."

"We'll park the moving van in the center of the garage at the mall. Then we will set up our band in the food court. After we perform a few songs, we hit the remote detonator and ka-boom. Here is a little bit of irony. That is the name of our group. Ka-boom."

He didn't know the half of it, or maybe he did. I'm posing as a singer. This is ironic as hell, me playing the part of Dee in a suicide mission. Eff me.

"I just had an amazing idea. We'll make your microphone the detonator, and you'll pull the trigger."

Like that, I went from being the human crystal ball to the human detonator.

"You're making a mistake, Hassan. Why kill these innocent people? It won't bring Hasheem back. And it won't save your soul."

"They are not innocent and my soul is already dead," he says coolly.

"I'm not a murderer," I say. "I won't kill, no matter what you do to me."

"We all have a point," he says "at which we become the thing we most detest."

CHAPTER TWENTY-TWO
Inevitable

I dream of raging fire. Trapped in the middle of a tunnel, I hold a tiny bundle in my arms, a soft white blanket, coated in ash. I race to the open mouth of the tunnel to find it blocked by flames shooting higher and higher. I turn and run the other way.

I hear music. I feel heat on my heels. Running toward the sound, I stop short of it. A band plays in a black hole. Their instruments are ablaze, but they play on, their charred bodies in flames. I want to leave. I ache to look away, but my feet melt to the ground.

A crying sound comes from inside the bundle I'm holding. I lift the corner of it and see the head of a microphone. The blanket falls away. The microphone starts ringing like a cell phone. I push a big red button to silence it and everything goes dark.

❖

"You're on, Janice. It's time for your solo," Hassan says through the door.

Covered in sweat, I wake up and sit bolt upright. I hear a baby crying. Even in a nursery filled with other babies, I'd know Jessie's plaintive cry. I leap out of the bed and pound on the door.

"Hassan! Hassan! Open this fucking door! You bastard! If you hurt her, I'll kill you! Do you hear me? I'll fucking kill you!"

The crying isn't constant. It starts, stops, and then starts all over again. As long as she's crying, she's still alive. He'd left me. I hear nothing now. I pound until I'm exhausted. I'm a puddle on the floor and hoarse from screaming. My knuckles are bleeding.

Then finally, the lock on the door releases.

❖

I had full faith in the lawyer duo of Brian and Alex. They sent me letters and emails filled with information that was Greek to me. While Brian explained the ins and outs of the law to me, I formed a plan to run away. After Jessie was born, I planned to take her to some place where Claire would never find us. Only how could I do this to Gram?

Finally, it was the big day, for bigger me, the day of the baby shower. On August 11, Jessie was a thirty-six-week-old human. Fully formed, she was growing stronger every day. Gram was surprisingly resilient. I believed she would actually beat the cancer.

"Well, look at all the cars. I never knew you were so popular Janice," Gram said as we drove through the parking lot of *Basilico*. I passed the vehicles of Cilla, Stefania, Annie, Mrs. S., the Fortini clan, Mel, and some of the Safe Harbor staff members. There was a sign in front of the spot closest to the door. It said, "Parking for the mother-to-be." We parked and watched Sue Hall, who was just walking into the restaurant.

"Who didn't they invite to this thing?" I asked Gram. Arm in arm, we strolled up the brick walkway. I was unsure if she was holding me up or if it was the other way around. At the entrance, an arch of pink and white balloons wiggled, tugging against their strings. Stefania and Cilla stood with big smiles under the balloons in the open doorway.

My heart was full. I had good friends. I had a new life. After everything I'd been through, I deserved some happiness in my life. It just wasn't going to be that day.

I felt myself go down like the sensation of falling in a dream. You try to catch yourself but instead you jolt awake. Only I wasn't dreaming. I was living a nightmare. I heard Cilla screaming, "Call 911. Janice, are you OK? Janice!"

Cilla and Stefania tried to lift me up off the ground, but I couldn't let go. "Gram, you can't do this now. I need you! I need you! Don't you get that?"

❖

I lived at the hospital for the next few days. The nurses insisted I stay there hooked up to monitors. They said that my stress might cause me to go into labor early. Gram never woke up again, but I felt she knew I was there holding her hand and praying.

Her doctor told me why she had stopped having appointments. The cancer had advanced too far. There was nothing to do but give her pain medication. The next day, she died quietly. She went the way everyone hopes to go but few ever do. Death isn't pretty. It's not peaceful. It's only inevitable.

❖

With the fork in my hand, I'm ready when Hassan opens the door. I lunge at him. He laughs, grabbing my wrists. He wrenches and twists my arms behind me, pinning me to the bed and lies on top of me.

"You little liar. I could snap you in two right now, but breaking your spirit is so much more entertaining."

I stare at him with blatant hate.

"It's like I said, Janice. Anyone can become a killer when the right button is pushed."

He kisses me, pressing his lips hard against mine. Bile rises in my mouth. I spit it out at him.

"Now you are ready."

❖

I'd never planned a funeral before. Thank God, I had my friends to lean on for support. The only family I'd ever known was gone. I met with Father Ballentine. He knew Gram as well as I did. He knew what to say and he knew what she would have wanted. The meeting was only for my benefit.

"You have her strength, Janice. You'll get through this, but I want you to know that we are all your family," he said.

"Thank you. I appreciate that."

"How are you doing with everything else?" He asked.

"Fine."

"Are you managing your visions through prayer?"

"Yes. It seems to be working. Why?" I asked.

"It's just that, um, I've known people who have turned to substances in times of stress," he said concerned.

"No," I said. "I'm good."

"Excellent," he said. "I have some news that I hope will lift your spirits some. Sister Bridget is opening a day care at the rectory. It's something your grandmother always wanted. We're naming it in her honor. It will be called the Beatrice Morrison Center."

It was a beautiful gesture. Gram would have been pleased. I sat there sobbing. She had sacrificed so much for me. Whatever it took, I was determined to make her proud of me.

❖

"Where is she?" I spat the words like venom at Hassan.

"Relax, Janice. I haven't done anything to the baby yet. I only took her voice. Here it is."

He placed a cell phone on the bed and pressed the ringtone button. It started to cry.

"Imagine," he said, "how close I had to get to capture that level of sound?"

CHAPTER TWENTY-THREE
Sympathy

*Blessed are they that mourn: for they shall
be comforted.* —Matthew 5:4, KJV

When I returned to my apartment, I found a mountain of pretty, pastel packages. While I'd been at the hospital, my friends had brought all of my shower gifts over. I walked over to the pile and kicked a pink, wrinkled balloon across the floor. I plucked out one of the gifts. Turning the box over in my hands, I guessed at the contents. It was a baby monitor to wake me when my baby cried out in the night.

Next to the presents was the rocker I'd registered for but with my last name etched in gold on the headrest: "Morrison." A squeezing tightness tugged at my belly. I ran my fingers over the occasionally cursed name that I would pass on to Jessie. The tag read:

Dear Janice,
Best wishes for the future. I have faith in you.
Love, Gram

Distracted by the new state of my apartment, I didn't realize I'd left the door open. Mrs. S. came up behind and hugged me.

"I'm so sorry, dear," she said. "What can I do? Are you hungry?"

"No," I said. "Thanks. I just need some sleep."

"Brian brought this for you," she said, handing me a letter. "OK. You sleep now. We filled your refrigerator and freezer to the brim with food from the party. When you get hungry, I'll warm something for you. OK? You get some rest."

I dragged myself to the bedroom and fell onto the bed. The letter was still in my hand. I didn't have any strength left for bad news. Then again, I couldn't fall much lower.

Claire modified the conditions of her lawsuit. She was now seeking partial custody of my baby. According to Brian, she had changed her mind in light of my grandmother's death. I guessed it was also in part due to his excellent negotiating skills. He advised me to accept this offer and move on with my life. There were worse possible outcomes.

"So, Gram, you're still looking after me?"

I let go of the letter. I let it float like a feather to the ground, and I slept like the dead.

❖

After dinner, Hassan ordered me to take my final shower. I needed to prepare for our band's deadly performance the next day. I wondered why it was necessary to be clean for a suicide mission. I choked down my last meal, a simple sandwich and a glass of water.

What would become of Jessie? My premonitions had failed me. Like decaying leaves, remnants of my faith fell in tatters around my heart. I'd fooled myself about this thing disguised as a gift — it was really a curse. One evil deed could unravel all of the good things a person had ever done.

❖

I'd been staying at Gram's cottage and making funeral arrangements. My apartment was still a mess of baby gifts. Since people kept calling the cottage to offer their condolences, it seemed rude not to be there. In case anyone decided to stop by after the funeral, I worked to get everything at Gram's place in order.

I hadn't worked a full week at Safe Harbor all month. I hoped that Mel would actually keep me on.

There were always so many decisions to make when someone passed away, decisions left up to me. I asked Stefania and Mrs. Fortini to take charge of organizing and handling the gathering and meal in the rectory after the funeral. It was one less worry. I knew they'd bring enough food to feed a small country. Even though my friends, Father B., the Ladies Auxiliary and the Sisters of Mercy had been supportive and helpful, I still felt alone with the monumental task of burying my grandmother. I had yet to face the funeral.

I was up before the sunrise, watching the sun do battle with some rain clouds. I put on a dress from Stefania's hand-me-down bag. It was from her Aunt Maria, who was still mourning her husband, who had died in the war. It wasn't a perfect fit, but I didn't care. I never planned to wear it again.

Annie, my escort to the funeral home, knocked on the back door. Before the Mass, there was a private ceremony reserved for family members. In this case, it was Father Ballentine, Annie, my spiritual advisor, and me. On our way to church an hour later, I spotted it. It was faint at first, but an unmistakable spray of colored light, stretched across the sky over the Chesapeake Bay. Admiring that rainbow, I blessed myself and said, "Godspeed, Gram. Save me a seat in heaven."

Inside the church, the scent of incense hung in air, an organ moaned, and there was beautiful display of flowers. Every detail was complete. I held my head up high and braced myself on Annie's arm, trying not to dwell on my situation. Nine months pregnant, in a borrowed dress, I waddled down the center aisle. I passed by everyone in town. Jessie was kicking up a storm throughout the whole thing. Cilla and Ken were in the front row waiting for me. Stefania and her family stood behind me, rubbing my back for support. All I wanted was to get through the service.

Father Ballentine gave a beautiful eulogy to a full church. I felt eyes on me the whole time. Some of them were sympathetic. Some of them were full of pity. Some of them were something else. Most people understood what grief did to a person. Most people knew the history of the Morrison family, so maybe what happened the night before, at the wake, wasn't a shock. When Dee made her grand reappearance and I met my granddad for the first time.

❖

Hassan, Saif, and Ahmed are practicing loudly. It's a song by the Rolling Stones. It's something about the devil. I run the water, making it as hot as I can. A steam cloud fills the small room. I deserve to burn.

Faith means believing when there's no proof—when all hope is hopelessly lost. I drop to my knees. I feel the cold, hard tile on my bare legs. I pray and beg for answers.

Over the music, I hear a different noise outside. *Whir. Whir. Whir.* It sounds like the beating of electronic wings. I fly to the window. I rip and tear away the black paper. There's a man in the yard next door with a leaf blower. I bang on the window and push with all of my might, trying to pry it open. It won't budge.

Whir. Whir. Whir.

I bang harder. The piece of glass breaks away from its toothpaste caulk and hits the floor, shattering. I stick my hand out of the hole in the window, waving frantically.

Whir. Whir. Whir.

The bits of glass still stuck in the window frame cut like fangs into my wrist.

Whir. Whir. Pttftt. Scritch. Scritch. The blower stops. A voice calls out, "Hola?"

He sees my hand. Then the music stops. *Please. Not now. Not now. Please. Please.* The music starts up again, louder than before.

"Hola," the man says. "Is someone there?"

I hold up one finger, wagging it to stop him from coming any closer.

"*Sí, se pierda,*" he whispers.

I close my fist. I point my thumb up and my pinky down.

"*Diablo?*"

I waggle my finger, making the sign again. This time I turn my hand so that my closed fingers curve in and face the window.

"*Teléfono?*"

I give a thumbs-up sign and then I hold up four fingers.

"*Sì, un numero.*"

Scritch. Scritch. Scritch. Scritch. I hear the rake.

I close my fist and hold up four fingers again. The rake answers me. Then I hold up three fingers, then two, five, and four. Hassan begins pounding on the door.

"Janice, I told you never to lock this door!"

I take a deep breath and hold up one finger, then one finger again and once more. Hassan pounds harder still.

Bang! Bang!

Now he's kicking in the door.

Bouf! Bouf!

The door buckles under the force of his kicks. I hold my hand steady and draw the last digit in the air, infinity, a figure eight.

Scritch. Scritch. Scritch. Scritch. Scritch. Scritch. Scritch. Scritch.

I wave. I motion with my middle and pointer fingers so they look like legs that are walking. I am telling him to run away. Staring at the door, I pull in my bleeding wrist and hand. The door whines and cracks. His booted foot is visible now.

I slump to the tile floor. I grab a piece of broken glass, drag it across my wrist, and tear open my vein. The door collapses and everything goes dark.

❖

Back in the room, Hassan changes the dressing on my wound. He's looking at the bandage, not at me.

"Janice, you work in the medical field. I know that you know that if you really want to commit suicide," he says, using his finger to demonstrate, he draws a cross on my arm, "you cut the arm this way—not this way. This is group suicide. There will be no more cheating. I do not want any more drama. My heart cannot take it, and you nearly put us off schedule. You should rest. We leave in the morning."

Rest? Not likely. I've laid all of my faith on a yard worker. I can only wait and hope that help is on the way.

❖

In all of my years with her, Gram never talked about her ex-husband. She didn't have a single photograph of him. I was unprepared when he walked up and gave me a big bear hug. I thought he was another overly friendly townie. I stiffened up like a bulging board with my arms stuck out at my sides. Like walruses greeting each other on the ice, our two bellies got in the way.

"Well, I guess the peach doesn't fall too far from the peach tree after all," he said, looking at my stomach.

"Do I know you, sir?" I asked, annoyed. He obviously knew Dee, who hadn't yet bothered to show up or even call. If there were worse insults, I wasn't aware of any.

"What a thing to say to your granddaddy."

I took a giant step backward. He had the gall to be offended, the man who had taken off years ago with some tart and never heard from again. At least this was the story that went around town. Even when Gram didn't tell me things, I heard about them anyway.

"I see. Well, thanks for coming," I said. He was tall and wide with a shock of white hair and a full beard, like a cheap Santa Claus at the mall. He had one of those string ties on, and he wore a gray suit with a pair of black cowboy boots.

"There's no need to be so formal," he said, smiling. "I suppose you get that from Beatrice." He smelled of day-old booze, and it was all I could do to keep my dinner down. Certain smells magnified during pregnancy. This man was like another bad spin on the genetic wheel. Boozy Cowboy Santa's blood was swimming through my veins.

A woman in her sixties sidled up to him. Her bright blue eye shadow clashed with her crimson blouse, which showed an inappropriate amount of cleavage. Her skin reminded me of the homemade, dried apples that Gram used to put in my kindergarten lunchbox.

"This is my wife, Sally. She's your step-grandma."

"Sally." I nodded with as little warmth as I could muster. Step-grandma, of all the nerve, "Would you please excuse me?"

Walking away, I heard Sally say, "Well, Al, I hope she doesn't drop her baby in the aisle on her way up to the casket tomorrow."

To say I was furious would be an understatement. I had to clench my jaw shut to hold back my tongue. I kept telling myself, "For Gram's sake, don't make a scene." I might have even been successful if things had remained at that level.

Cilla planted herself by my side throughout the night, as a long line of people offered their condolences. I truly appreciated all of the kindness that these people had shown, but I was exhausted. My ankles swelled from standing for so long. Jessie was heavy. I locked my hands under my stomach, using them as a sling of support.

Gram's friends from church came through the line, along with the relatives of people whose funerals Gram had attended over the years, which comprised most of the town. Mel and my Safe Harbor coworkers came, as well as Mrs. S., Brian, Alex, Sheila, Sheila's daughters, Stefania, and Mr. and Mrs. Fortini. I saw the rest of the Fortini family dispersed in groups including Maximus, Ciro, and Enzo. Finally, I saw Francesco.

"Janeeze," he said hugging me, "I'm so sorry for you. You have suffered so much."

He kissed my cheeks and I began to cry. If he had scooped me up and carried me away from there, I would have never looked back and without regret. The line continued after him and I had my duty to complete the task of accepting everyone's condolences. Francesco's cologne clung to my dress and kept me company throughout the night whenever my spirit threatened to fail.

When the line dwindled down to a handful of kind souls, the back door creaked open. There she was the prodigal daughter. Dee brought up the end of the line in a royal-blue dress, cut so low and hemmed so high that the only thing the imagination wanted was more dress. In her spiked high heels, she stood a little taller than I did.

Gram, what would you have me do about all of my poor white-trash relatives who are coming out of the woodwork like a bunch of cockroaches. They seem a little too cheerful for a funeral.

"How are you holding up, baby?" Dee asked.

Cilla, with eyes as wide as saucers and mouth agape, looked Dee up and down.

"Cilla," I said. "Would you mind getting me some water? This heat's going straight to my head."

"Sure thing, Janice. Ms. Morrison, would you like—"

"She's fine," I answered for Dee. "She won't be staying." I crossed my arms and kept my eyes fixed on Dee. "I'm hardly a baby, Dee. I'll be twenty-one this month."

"Well, there's something to celebrate!" Dee shrieked. "Maybe we should have a party."

"Right," I said. "A party would be so appropriate. Won't you be leaving tomorrow to crawl back under the rock you came out from?" It was mean-spirited and she'd had it coming for fifteen years.

"Janice honey, it wasn't my idea not to see you. It was that witch. She threw me out of your life! I have to say, I'm not sorry she's gone. She made my life a living hell."

If blood could boil, mine would have been a bloody volcano. I thought about what Gram had said about never losing your temper in an unladylike fashion and always being gracious and polite. I thought about it, but I also thought that Gram might understand how it was sometimes too hard to be well mannered. I grabbed Dee's arm and pulled her toward the exit door.

"You're not welcome here. Get out!" I said, holding the door open.

She planted her feet, put her hands on her hips and smugly said, "Janice, I understand you're upset, sweetie. You loved her. I get that, but you can't throw me out of my own mother's wake. Besides, we're going to be roomies for a while. You may as well get used to the idea of having me around—at least until I get what's coming to me."

I erupted. *Whack!* I slapped her hard across the face. It made such a loud sound that the few remaining folks in the funeral parlor fell instantly silent.

"There," I said. "Now you've finally gotten what's been coming to you."

She lunged at me with both of her arms swinging.

"You little bitch!" she shouted.

I staggered backward, my pregnant self less graceful than normal and nearly fell over. Cilla came running. The glass of water in her hand was sloshing all over. The funeral director jumped between Dee and me. I took the glass from Cilla and tossed the water over the director's shoulder, hitting Dee square in the face.

Dee made an inhuman sound. She was swinging so wildly that one of her high heels flew straight across the room. To stave off the attack, the director held Dee around her waist. Cilla jumped in front of me, protecting the belly. It was quite a scene.

"Ma'am," the director said, catching his breath. "I'm going to have to ask you to leave."

Dee shrieked as he carried her toward the door. "This isn't over! You don't know the half of it!"

I stood there steely-eyed and watched her go. I foolishly hoped that it would be the last I'd see of Dee, but I knew better, of course. If Gram hadn't been rolling over before, she surely was now. I felt terrible about the whole thing only because it was a disgrace to Gram. I vowed to keep my cool the next day at the funeral.

Cilla saw that I got home safe. I double bolted the cottage door in case Dee showed up on the doorstep.

If Dee was at the funeral, I never saw her. It was blissfully drama free as was the meal afterward. I spent more time with Francesco than some people deemed appropriate as I could tell by all the whispering. I no longer cared about what people said. Afterward, I went back to my own apartment. I was beyond whatever was supposed to come after exhaustion. I had all sorts of pain in my back and sides.

I had yet to sort out Gram's possessions, but I decided that it could certainly wait for another day. All I had brought with me was her paperwork. I set it aside and slept. The next day was my birthday, even though I thought I'd never look forward to celebrating it again.

I woke up feeling achy still, but I was determined to get my apartment sorted out and open all of Jessie's presents. When I finished, Jessie had everything in the world a new baby could need, including a mother who was anxiously awaiting her arrival.

Happy Birthday, Janice.

The only thing missing was a crib. I looked over at my dresser drawer and called Cilla. "I just wanted to thank you for everything you've done for me over the past few weeks. I never could have made it through without you."

"That's what friends are for," she said. "So, have you heard from her?"

"No," I said. "Thank the Lord. You have to come over and see all of the beautiful baby things. I can't believe I missed my own shower."

"I know," Cilla said. "I'm so sorry, Janice."

"Thanks. You know, I don't think I need one thing, other than a crib. I can keep my eye open at the thrift stores after the baby's born."

"When I bought my gift, I saw on the registry that someone had bought the crib," Cilla said.

"What?" I asked. "Who was it?"

"I don't know, but I imagine it will be delivered."

"That's not possible," I said. "I made a list of everything everyone gave me. I kept track so I could write my thank-you notes. There's no one left."

"It must be some mysterious guardian angel," Cilla said.

"It must be."

CHAPTER TWENTY-FOUR
Engagement

Brian and Alex agreed to help me with all of the legal paperwork I had to handle after Gram passed away. They joined me in my meeting with Gram's executor, who was a man from the bank. I owed Brian and Alex so much already. I had no idea how I'd ever repay them.

According to the executor, Gram had left me the house, all of its contents, her car, and all of the funds from her bank account.

"The only issue," the man said, "is that the will is being contested."

"Contested by whom?" Brian asked.

"Mr. Alan Gerald Morrison and Ms. Deirdre Morrison," he said.

Also known as Boozy Cowboy Santa and Slutty Dee, who Gram had left nothing and who thought they were entitled to it all.

"Mr. Morrison is claiming a right to the house, and Ms. Morrison is claiming to be the only legal heir," he added.

What a laugh! The house was Gram's and hers alone. He went on.

"Ms. Morrison might have a case, but there's nothing to Mr. Morrison's claims. In fact, after their divorce he owed child support that was never paid. From a legal standpoint, Beatrice was the only person listed on the deed to the property. It's currently free and clear of all liens, including a home-improvement loan that was taken over twenty-five years ago and paid in full over a ten-year period."

Son of a bleep! Rumor had it that Al had forged Gram's signature on the loan, right before skipping town. He blew all of the money on gambling.

"Anyway, Miss Morrison, I informed the petitioners and gave each of them documents to sign. These documents ask them to relinquish their claims based on the contents of the will. Most of the time, people comply so that they will avoid creating additional grief and expenses. I haven't heard anything yet. As a matter of procedure, all of the assets will remain frozen for six months, but it could extend beyond that timeframe."

I had faith that two lawyers and a smart banker could get it sorted out. I had never planned to live in the cottage without Gram. Being there for the last few days had been depressing enough. I sure as hell wouldn't let Boozy or the Floozy have it, though. I planned to donate most of Gram's things. Her old Lincoln and the religious items would go to The Sisters of Mercy.

I went straight from the meeting to the cottage, relieved Dee had found some other place to sleep. Still, I'd made a colossal mistake by leaving the house unguarded. Someone had stripped it bare. All of the furniture was gone. Even the curtains were missing. Someone had ransacked the kitchen. The cabinets lay open, emptied of dishes, pots, and pans. There was a space on the counter where the microwave oven had been, marked by a rectangular dust outline. Every, last picture had been removed from the walls.

They only things left behind were the stove, the old television set, and the avocado refrigerator. They had likely planned to come back for these items. Maybe they needed another truck. If I had been in a normal state of mind before the funeral, I'd have called a locksmith to change the locks.

I walked into the chapel. All of Gram's statues and religious items were absent. If I didn't do something, they'd likely end up on eBay or in some yard sale. I knew well who the culprits were and it was just a matter of tracking them down.

I could say I felt disgusted, appalled, or sickened. There were no words left in my arsenal strong enough to describe what Al and Dee had done. I slipped outside and went back to the one-car garage. Sure enough, the car was gone. I was past steaming. Stealing a car intended for the nuns was an all time low even for Dee.

I went back inside and called the cops. Then I bent to pick up the small TV with the intention of taking it with me. The most heinous pain shot through my body. If I wasn't dying, I wanted to die in order to end the pain.

If Jessie had any chance of escaping the drama of the Morrison women, it ended with her full police escort to the hospital with sirens ablaze.

During the birth, I sobbed like a baby. I just couldn't hold back the sadness anymore. The nurse thought I was crying about the pain, but I wasn't. It hurt like hell, but I wasn't about to give Dr. Williams the satisfaction of saying, "I told you so." I looked him straight in the eyes and said, "Remember, I want no drugs."

I managed to make it through, even though I felt like a wishbone cracking in two when Jessie finally ventured down the birth canal. Cilla made it to the delivery room seconds before the newcomer, Jessica Beatrice Morrison, was born. Jessie's middle name would surely cause of one of the many difficulties I'd create for my young daughter. What could I do? I had to honor Gram.

The thing I'm most sorrowful about is that Gram and Jessie never met. I've read that when one soul leaves the earth abruptly and another is born soon thereafter, the old soul jumps straight into the new baby. I like to think Jessie has Gram's soul now. It was a good one.

Jessie's birth lit a fire in Cilla that I'd never seen before. Poor Ken never had a chance. They announced their engagement.

After receiving a parade of visitors later, I felt relieved to go home to my quiet apartment with my new roommate, who was sound asleep and wrapped like a sausage in her receiving blanket. On her head, she wore a hand knit cap. One of the senior citizen's from Safe Harbor had donated her time and talent to making it.

I stared at her in amazement.

The door buzzer rang. Having seen the whole cast of characters at the hospital, I wasn't expecting anyone else. I opened the door to a delivery truck driver and Claire.

"Where would you like it, miss?" the man asked.

"Where would I like what?" I said, trying to wrap my brain around the fact that Claire was at my apartment.

"The baby's nursery, of course," Claire said.

"We're sharing the bedroom," I said, pointing to the only other room in my apartment. The man carted in boxes and tools with a hand truck, and he set to work building the crib. It was the beautiful white one with the matching bedding.

"Janice, I was very sorry to hear about your grandmother," Claire said.

"Thank you," I said.

Jessie required feeding every two hours. I was too tired to do battle with Claire. New mother tired was a foggy sensation. You'd wander around between half-asleep and half-awake, never certain if you could maintain either for very long. I felt worn as thin as a pane of glass that any strong wind could easily shatter.

"Janice, I wanted you to know that I've dropped the lawsuit entirely."

"Oh," I said. "Why?"

"May I?" she asked, walking toward me and opening her hands to take Jessie.

"Sure." I tentatively handed Jessie over, careful not to wake her. My arms fought the urge to snatch her back.

Claire walked to the window, smiling down at Jessie and rocking her in her arms. She looked out. The light reflected on her face, softening it. She talked more to the trees than to me.

"Jason's mother was a troubled girl. We had some issues to overcome when he was a baby. He was born with addiction. He had some behavioral problems in his youth, but a mother's instinct is to always protect her child."

She looked at me. "You've surprised me, Janice. You're a strong young woman. I know you'll take good care of her."

I nodded, at a loss for words.

"I wanted a little girl so desperately. Unfortunately, it was not to be. We felt blessed to have found Jason," she said. "He leaves for medical school this week, and I'll have some extra time on my hands. I hope you'll consider allowing me to watch Jessica for you every now and then."

"Sure," I said. "I imagine we can work something out."

While Claire and I were having the first real conversation we ever had, the man building the crib finished and left. Claire carefully handed Jessie back to me.

"I'll be on my way," she said. "I'm sure you need your rest. If there's anything you need for Jessica, please let me know."

"Thank you, Claire."

❖

Dee was still in town. The police had picked her up at the Snake Bite Bar in North Beach after spotting Gram's stolen car in the lot. It had been stacked to the brim with Gram's worldly possessions.

They found Dee perched at the bar, pounding shots. She was complaining to anyone who would listen about how her own mother had threatened to have her committed and caused her to run away. Worse, she claimed Gram had stolen me, her only daughter, and turned me into an ungrateful little bitch.

Jody, the bartender, was my former classmate. After the fact, she gave me the entire sordid story. I was secretly glad the cops showed Dee no mercy. One of them, Jake Stevens, Dee had screwed over in high school. The other, Frank Heller, went to Saint Mary's with Gram and me. I loved karma. The pair of them dragged her off the bar stool by her hair. She put up such a fight it took the two of them to cart her out of the bar. Someone got the whole thing on video, but I sure as heck didn't want to see it. It was probably a big hit on YouTube, though.

The ironic thing was that Dee had no one to bail her out the next day. Boozy Cowboy Santa had already skipped town with the moving van full of furniture. Disappearing was his specialty, after all. Of all people, they called me to get her out after I was the one who put her in there. Jake said that it would serve her right if I just let her rot.

I know now when God is testing me. I know that he wanted me to search my heart and soul for forgiveness. I did search. I just couldn't muster any up.

"Sorry, Lord," I said. "Forgiveness will have to be one of those things I strive for later in life. You have my apologies, this simply isn't the time."

Dee was pathetic. She was sitting in her cell bawling with makeup running down her face, clothes disheveled, and her hair sticking out in all directions. She reminded me of one of those old burnt-out hookers you see in bad movies.

"Janice, darlin', will you at least send me a picture of my new grandbaby? I can leave you my address, in case you ever want to get in touch with me."

"I don't see any reason why I'd need to," I answered, unmoved. "Maybe I'll give you a call in fifteen years."

Even though she had it coming, I felt somewhat guilty about being a proper shit. She was so pitiable. I signed the paperwork, paid her bail, and left without looking back.

As a sort of compromise, I dropped the charges on the condition that Dee would return everything she'd stolen. She also had to drop any notion of fighting the will. Furthermore, she had to obey the restraining order I'd taken out against her, which stated that she was not to be within five hundred feet of Jessie, Gram's house, or me. I know it was about as far away from forgiveness as a person can get, but I never claimed to be perfect.

According to Jake, Al, aka Boozy, had rented the U-Haul locally. I could've had him arrested as well, but I was tired of the whole business at that point. I wrote it off as a loss. It saved me the pain of cleaning the place out before putting it up for sale down the line. Brian and Alex tracked Al down, and the threat of arrest was enough to get him to sign away any claims. I had my eyes fixed on my future with Jessie. I couldn't let negativity sway me.

❖

Months later, the Sisters were thrilled with the car and the religious statues. I only kept the one I'd given Gram last Christmas.

Life had normalized somewhat for me after all of the madness. I focused on my new routine of feeding, diapering, and mothering Jessie while she and I grew accustomed to one another. I was busy with work, spending time with my friends and seeing Francesco and his family whenever it was humanly possible.

Francesco was busy working at *Basilico* and for Stefania's catering business. He complained about Stefania's bossiness, but by all accounts, her business was a huge success with a surprise investor, Claire O'Neil. Claire's way of keeping Stefania working for her was to loan Stefania the money for a catering van and to help promote Stefania's business among her wealthy friends.

The Sisters of Mercy were my angels on earth, always there to help with Jessie's care. I set up a babysitting arrangement with Claire where she cared for Jessie some nights. Like a normal twenty-one year-old, I went on dates with Francesco and Jessie received love from so many directions.

It's funny how much a year can change your life. At twenty, I was a child thinking only of myself and meandering through life without any real direction. By twenty-one, I'd become a full-fledged mothering adult.

CHAPTER TWENTY-FIVE
Detonator

*Blessed are the meek: for they shall inherit
the earth.* —Matthew 5:5, KJV

In the morning, we'll leave for the mall to set the stage for our final act. I don't hear anyone stirring. The television's been off for hours. I haven't been able to sleep, hoping, praying and willing my eyes to stay open. Now my lids drop like shades. I'm ready to give in to the end of the light.

❖

"Come, on! We don't have much time."

I'm dreaming. I must be. I expect to hear Hassan's voice, but I hear another instead.

"Janeeze, wake up! Come on. Wake up!"

Two figures wearing black clothes and ski masks are standing over me. Their brown, familiar eyes show through the slits in the masks. Nocturnal bandits answered my call and I'm the treasure they'll whisk away in the night while my captors sleep.

"Grazie a Dio," Francesco says. "We were so worried. We didn't know what happened to you. Do you know how long we've looked for you?"

I honestly don't know.

"Come on. Come on," Stefania hisses. "They'll wake up,"

They carry me out of the room like a drunk with my arms draped over their shoulders. We make our way toward the front door. Passing through the living room, I count the bodies of the men on the floor, scattered like rugs between the instrument cases. Saif, Ahmed, and Muhammad had been packing up and getting ready before the gas leaked inside.

Through a thin tube, my friends had sent the gas into the hole in the bathroom window. Like ninjas, Ciro and Enzo bend over the men who held me hostage here. With rope, the ninjas bind the feet and hands of my kidnappers.

"Ciro, Enzo," Francesco says, "go through the woods to the car. Max is waiting."

Groggy, I ask, "Where's the fourth one?"

"What do mean?" Francesco says. "There were only three of them."

"No!" I shout, wondering where Hassan is hiding. I slip away from them and stagger back toward the garage.

"Janeeze, no," Francesco pleads. "They'll wake up soon."

"Janeeze," Stefania calls after me. "We have to leave. We have to call the police."

"Where is she going?" Francesco asks Stefania.

The moving van is still in the garage. Where's Hassan? They had another vehicle, the utility van. Adrenalin pumping, I'm wide-awake now. I fly past the others to the front window. The van isn't outside. My mind's racing. I'll never be free. He'll hunt me like an animal.

"Janeeze, we're leaving." Forcefully, Stefania grabs my arm and pulls me out of the house. The outside air feels foreign against my skin. I look back. The living room light glows eerily against the night sky. For the first time, I see the small brick house that was my prison. I'm free.

The brick house and the dark shape of the empty house next door sit alone on the gravel road, surrounded by woods. I go with my friends toward the woods behind the house. Stefania tells me her small gray car is hidden and waiting for us. I can't see anything in the darkness, but I have faith.

Then, I remember my journal. If I leave it, the police will find it. I can't take that risk. They might think I'm involved with the terrorists somehow. I turn away from Stefania and run back to the house.

"Janeeze! What are you doing?" Stefania screams.

"Wait for me," I tell her.

Running so hard that my heart wants to burst, I push the door open and step past the men on the floor. I search around, sifting through everything in my path, until I see my journal on the kitchen counter. I grab the journal and stuff it down the front of my drawstring pants.

Tires crunch on the gravel. They must have pulled up in front of the house to get me. I run to the front door and someone is waiting there, blocking my exit. It's not one of my friends. Over his shoulder, I see the white van. In the doorway, Hassan and I are face to face for a moment.

"Going somewhere, Janice? I told you, if one of us goes, we all go."

He strikes out with his fist and knocks me to the floor. My head pounding, I taste blood on my lip. I've failed. Where are my friends? Did they see Hassan? Did he see them? Did they get away? Hassan drags me by the ankles into the living room and leaves me lying in a heap while he squats to check on the others, still unconscious but breathing.

"I am impressed," he says, "that you were able to do all of this in my absence. How did you do it? Did you give them the sleeping pills that I've been giving you?"

I fight to keep my eyes open, to watch Hassan. He's examining the rope that binds the men.

"No," he says, narrow-eyed. "You had help. Where are they?" He thinks my friends are hiding in the house and begins searching. Where did they go? How did he not see them? Did they leave me? Finding no one, he returns. He reaches down and pulls a sheath from Ahmed's belt. He withdraws the knife from the sheath and goes outside to search some more.

Focus. Pray. Get up Janice.

My breathing is labored, either from the blow or from panic. I hear him outside the house, crunching through the leaves. Then, he opens the van doors. When he returns, he walks across the living room, over to the keyboard.

My eyes are blurry, watery now. My left eye won't open all of the way. The knife is back in its sheath, clipped to his belt. I blink hard and see him pick up the microphone. He checks it and then slips it into his back pocket.

The detonator.

He moves to the first instrument case, stepping over me like I'm road-kill.

"The cowards have left, Janice. I guess you chose the wrong friends."

He loads an instrument case and lugs it out to the van. I close my eyes and concentrate on breathing while darkness settles over me. I have one chance left to make things right.

If I go, you go.

He returns and bends down with his back to me, packing the next case. I drag myself to a crawling position and move slug-like across the floor. I push up and snatch the microphone from his back pocket. He spins, glaring at me and then starts to laugh.

With his face inches away from mine, he says, "Go ahead, Janice. Blow us all to Allah. I'm ready to go. Are you?"

I grip the microwave and press it's only button, hard. Closing my eyes, I wait for the explosion that doesn't come.

"Do you honestly think I would trust you with the trigger? You must think I'm an idiot."

Standing above me, he kicks me hard in the stomach, knocking the wind out of me. I let the microphone drop and curl into a ball on the floor. Ahmed, Saif, and Muhammad start moving, wriggling around on the floor like eels. It's over.

"It's show time," Hassan says picking me up and tossing me over his shoulder. He carries me out of the house and toward the van. Upside down, I see light at the base of the trees. In the glow of the rising sun, a shadowy figure creeps toward the back of the house.

I won't let Hassan hurt anyone else. I grab the knife handle and rip it from his belt. Reaching back to stop me, he lets go of me, dropping me onto the ground. I nearly stab myself with the knife. He lunges at me, grabbing my wrist, but misses the one holding the knife. When he twists my arm, I plunge the knife deep into his stomach, turning it.

Wild eyed, he gasps and looks down. I stare up at him, shocked at what I've done. He clutches his shirt, pressing his hands around the shaft of the knife into the blood that flows from his wound. Anatomy 101, I know where all of the vital organs are. He stands staring down in disbelief. I scramble to my feet and run.

My legs are lead weights I force to move against their will. I hear Francesco calling my name, running from behind the house. Stefania's car moves quickly up the street towards us. Francesco grabs me, tugging me toward the car.

We're almost there when I hear a sound that stops me cold. The sound makes me hesitate even when I know I should keep running. I look at Francesco, my savior, and then and I look back toward the sound of Jessie's cry.

Hassan still standing where I left him, has one bloody arm up in the air, a cell phone in his hand. His eyes fixed on me, he pushes a button and the crying stops. I say a quick protection prayer for my friends and for myself before a wave of heat lifts my body into the air, and I fly like an angel.

❖

When I woke up in the hospital, I was sure it was heaven. Everything was so bright and white. Annie, Stefania and Cilla kept constant vigil at my side and when I was well enough, Bridge brought Jessie to me. I cried not because she'd grown so much in the few weeks I was gone, but because in that short time she didn't know me anymore. She clung on to Bridge, as if Bridge was her real momma.

"It's okay," I said, rubbing her small back. "We have our whole lives to get to know each other."

Since I was stuck in the hospital with a concussion, severe burns on my hands and feet and minor cuts and abrasions, I missed the Fortini Christmas party. By some miracle, Stefania and her cousins were fine, but Francesco suffered minor injuries when the bomb exploded. By all accounts, we should all be dead. Go figure.

Francesco's room was on a different floor of the hospital than mine, but he'd managed to make friends with all of the nurses on both floors so they overlooked his constant visits to my room.

Cilla had kept a complete record of all of the newspaper clippings and had recorded the news coverage of my kidnapping. It was the most excitement the town had seen in years.

I wept when I saw the picture of Jessie with the caption, "Missing Mother Leaves Infant." The article speculated about my whereabouts and included quotes from various townspeople. Some people suggested that I'd skipped town. I had a family history of this kind of behavior. The story went into Dee's lifelong antics, ending with her recent arrest.

My favorite was the quote from Mel Golden. She said, "Janice is my best employee. She's a responsible, hard worker and a good mother. I don't believe for a second that she left of her own free will. Something happened to her. The police should be looking for suspects."

The article went on to quote others on their opinions about my character. Claire O'Neil, a prominent citizen and my former employer, said, "It is unimaginable that the North Beach Police Department still has no leads." Mrs. O'Neil had offered a reward for any information leading to my whereabouts. She had hired her own private detective, but his investigation had not led to my rescue.

I thought about the landscaper who was raking the leaves. Did he know that he'd saved my life?

It was surreal to read about myself like this. The news covered an evening vigil led by the Sisters of Mercy. They had also broadcast the exhaustive search efforts, and they showed Sue Hall handing out free meals from the parking lot of Bayside Diner for everyone involved in the search.

Divers searched the Chesapeake Bay and the surrounding waterways. They found a bicycle, some car tires, a pair of work boots, a gun, multiple fishing rods and various animal skeletons, but they found no sign of me.

By the end of the second week, the search efforts had dwindled down to my nearest and dearest friends. Cilla and Ken had posted flyers with my picture on them all over the county and handled the resulting calls. Stefania and Annie stayed on top of the police investigation. Francesco and the boys went door to door, driving up and down the county.

Dee and her band, the Dee-Lights, hosted a benefit concert on the boardwalk in North Beach, but there were questions about where the money ended up. Typical Dee.

After her stay in Safe Harbor, Mrs. S. moved to Alexandria to live with Sheila. The doctors expected she would make a full recovery.

Finally, there was an article about the boating accident in Deale. It had nearly claimed the lives of Annie, and her friends. They had managed to swim to safety, counting their blessings as they watched her beloved sailboat sink to the bottom of the bay.

I refused to give a statement to anyone but Sheila and the FBI. My journal partially destroyed in the blast, I could have told Shelia anything, but I opted for the truth.

The story Sheila told to the press was fiction. In the press conference, she stated that a recluse had captured me. She said that he had held me against my will in an abandoned house in Northern Virginia. I had narrowly escaped during a freak gas explosion and my captor died resulting from the accident.

She told me something that I hadn't thought through before then.

"Janice, the kinds of people who do these types of things are often part of large, intricate networks."

"OK," I said. I wasn't getting it.

"We have no way of knowing how far this terror cell reaches. We don't know how much information might be out there about you."

"OK." I still wasn't getting it.

"Janice, what I'm saying is that this part of your nightmare might be over, but you're not completely out of danger. We need to conduct a further investigation. You'll have to cooperate with the FBI and with other agencies. If you share any of this with anyone, you could put yourself and others at risk."

"What about after that? When can I live a normal life again?" I asked.

"Janice, I'm sorry," she said. "You'll likely never live a normal life."

❖

Five months later, my life is in order, so to speak. I sold Gram's cottage, gave up my apartment and moved into a townhome by the Chesapeake Bay, where Jessie has her own room. I met with Gram's financial advisor at the bank. Using the money Nanny had left me, I opened a college fund for Jessie.

I also registered for a few classes of my own. Thanks to Sheila, I decided on a major, linguistics. I figured I could learn some new skills that would be valuable to certain agencies in the district. My unique talent for predicting terrorist attacks has already proven valuable for work on special projects for some of those agencies. I kept my part-time job at Safe Harbor. It's a good cover.

After the move, I sorted through Gram's paperwork and discovered a few things, including a passbook with twenty thousand dollars in savings or better known as the Janice Morrison Scholarship fund. I also found a medal of Saint Joseph, a patron saint of marriage. I gave it to Cilla as an early wedding gift.

The most surprising find was a pink diary, authored by sixteen-year-old Deirdre Morrison. I popped it open and read the whole thing from cover to cover. Anyone else might have thought that this girl was crazy, but I knew better. One passage I read repeatedly.

Dear Diary,   June 4, 1992
She's going to lock me up and take away my baby.
I know she sees things and hears things too,
but she just prays them away.
Drinking and smoking weed takes mine away.
Now that I'm pregnant, I shouldn't be drinking,
but if I'm not crazy already, being locked up will surely drive me crazy. All I have left is singing.
I can still sing the voices away.

For the first time ever, I felt sorry for Dee. When Jessie's time comes, I'll be there to teach her how to handle her gift. I'll teach her like Annie taught me.

The secret of my rescue created a special bond between me, Francesco and the Fortini family. I've never told the rest of my friends the real story of my kidnapping. Ken and I exchange knowing looks sometimes. He may or may not know, but he won't hear about anything from me. I've been helping Cilla with the last-minute arrangements for their wedding. Occasionally I'm tempted to tell her, especially when she asks things.

"What was the guy like? Weren't you terrified beyond belief?"

"Cilla, I'd rather just forget about it."

If only I could. I keep busy. There are days when I don't think about Hassan. There are days when my heart doesn't pound, and when I don't constantly look over my shoulder.

I went with Cilla to a bar in Annapolis to see the Dee-Lights. It was our last hurrah before the wedding in June. Dee was up on stage, belting out rock and roll tunes. Listening to her sing, I felt the hairs on the back of my neck stand straight up and the flood of harsh memories triggered by the song.

Forgetfulness is the privilege of an ordinary life.

Dee seemed both surprised and excited to see me. We actually had a civil conversation afterward where I told her she didn't completely stink as a singer. That's as far as I'll go toward forgiveness for now. It's a big step for me.

❖

Today I'm on vacation in Naples, Italy. Jessie is napping at the villa, surrounded by surrogate aunts and grandmothers and I'm spending time with Stefania and Francesco joyriding through the hillside along the bay of Naples. Stefania drives the convertible like a wild woman through the scenic countryside while Francesco sits with me in the backseat.

I never knew there were so many tunnels in Italy. As we pass through another one, I hold my breath. In the dark, Francesco squeezes my hand. I have no premonitions this time. When we come out on the other side, I see the warm sun and Francesco's chocolate-brown eyes as hot as the molten-lava cake I devoured after lunch.

As this vision, the one I had while locked in my closet prison, becomes a reality, I know now that I can trust my gift. After all, I am Janice Morrison, aka the Secret Agent of God.

The End-

Author Bio

Eileen Slovak is a former account executive turned writer. She received her bachelor of arts in English from the University of Rhode Island, and currently lives in Chesapeake Beach, MD.

The initial inspiration for *Secret Agent of God* came to Slovak while researching an article on ghosts she wrote for *The Bay Weekly Newspaper*. She lived in Italy for three years, and cared for elderly relatives, two experiences that influenced the development of the novel's characters.

More information on Eileen Slovak can be found on her Facebook page, or visit her website at www.eileenslovak.com.

Made in the USA
Middletown, DE
29 September 2023